# DEADLIEST OF THE SPECIES

BY JOHN LEE SCHNEIDER

SEVEREDPRESS

# DEADLIEST OF THE SPECIES



WWW.SEVEREDPRESS.COM



*ISBN: 978-1-922861-88-7*

*"When the Himalayan peasant meets the he-bear in his pride, he shouts to scare the monster, who will often turn aside. But the she-bear thus accosted rends the peasant tooth and nail, for the female of the species is more deadly than the male."*

*Rudyard Kipling*

**Timeline:** This tale takes place between **AGE OF MONSTERS** and **KINGDOM OF MONSTERS.**

# CHAPTER 1

Mark had been in the mountains two days, following a map, trying to navigate the Colorado Rockies. It was still early and the creeping sun hadn't yet chased away the morning chill.

He almost lingered in camp, a nice little cubbyhole cave in the rocks, where he'd spent the night – a lucky find, because it stormed hard last night. He sat, nestled safe from the elements, and had even been able to light a small fire. The wind kept the smoke out of his eyes.

His little makeshift burrow lay along an overgrown logging route. It was tough going – the road was steep, and there were no longer any work crews clearing the way.

This was new territory, and Mark was grateful for the night's respite. He was tempted to camp a few days, perhaps rebuild his supplies for the rest of the trip over the mountain. It was late summer, so the snows were gone except near the peaks, but there was still rough travel ahead, and a long way to go.

Mark was going home.

He hadn't even been gone that long, barely a year and a half. But he knew it was going to a lot different than when he left it.

It had been a *big* eighteen months.

Ironically, Mark actually missed most of it – one of the benefits to being in military custody, where he'd been ever since he and Sally were *'rescued'*, after the sinking of the *Pacific Princess*.

He and Sally.

Mark felt the familiar sting every time he let himself think her name.

KT-day was eleven months ago, almost a year. The whole world had been lost that day. But Mark was coming to terms with *that*.

He lost Sally six weeks ago. The grief was still quite fresh.

So now he was going home.

He knew very well what he would find. He'd seen it all on close-circuit military TV.

There were no safe-zones on KT-day. Mark had to reluctantly admit being in custody was probably what saved his life.

Now that he was out on the open road, it was startling to see the sheer totality of destruction.

At first, he thought there really *was* no one left. As hard a species as humans might be to eradicate, Mark was having doubts.

For better or worse, the following weeks proved him wrong. Stragglers maintained, and Mark quickly learned, in the new modern world, contact with your fellow-man was not necessarily a good thing.

Over the last six weeks, there were two attempted robberies and, once, someone had taken a shot at him. He never saw who, and never knew why.

Now he was seeing signs of human habitation again.

And even before he'd hit the mountain trail, he felt that subtle sixth-sense kicking in – that odd, crawly feeling of being *watched.*

It was a sensation that was becoming uncomfortably familiar, and Mark *always* listened to those unruly hairs when they popped up on the back of his neck. He'd spent more than one night in a tree, and *that* had most assuredly saved his life.

It was a wild world these days.

He spent ten-minutes breaking camp, kicked out his small fire, and headed down the road.

Along the way, he saw some of the brush was cleared – more human activity.

Perhaps there was a settlement ahead. He would have to be careful, lest they not be receptive to strangers.

A little further on, he came across bits of refuse that looked fresh. Scraps of cloth littered the clearing, looking oddly out of place in the overgrowth.

Humans still despoiling the environment.

Mark picked up a foul-smelling piece of torn towel. It smelled like it had been used to clean-up skunk-piss. He tossed it aside distastefully, wiping his hands against his pants.

He hiked-up his pace. Something about the area was giving him the creeps. Those familiar neck-hairs were standing on full-alert.

So far, he'd seen no evidence the locals were any more than litterbugs, but he wanted to get clear of the territory.

But as he rounded the next bend, the sight that greeted him brought him to a full-stop.

Standing in the middle of the road, its nose to the ground, was a full-grown *Tyrannosaurus rex*.

Mark could hear the rasp of the beast's breath as it sniffed along the path. It growled at another of those rank-smelling rags, apparently displeased by the stench.

Then it reared up, cocking its head in that oddly bird-like fashion, and turned to stare directly at him.

"Oh, *shit*," Mark said.

He turned and ran.

# CHAPTER 2

It was a good thing Mark had a head start. Even a big rex could outrun a human on flat ground – a fact for which Mark could bear direct witness.

They were damn stubborn too.

Behind him, the foghorn blast of the rex' roar shook the trees, and Mark felt the Earth shake as heavy footsteps thundered after him.

Rexy was on his trail again.

She had probably been stalking him all morning. Ten minutes earlier, and she would have caught him still camped. Luckily, the wind was against her. But now her quarry had been flushed, and all that was left for Mark was to beat hell.

The big rex was a smart one, too. Just like captive crocodiles Mark had seen on the Nature Channel, coming after their keepers at feeding time – once from one angle, the next day from another, plotting and planning, trying new tricks. Rexy was like *that*.

But there was an important difference – a croc was a *reptile*, with limited energy, and if it missed the initial strike, you could probably evade it.

Rexy had a physiology more like a five-ton ostrich. She wasn't going to get tired. At least, not before *you* did.

And bullets were damn near useless. Mark had tried a wide array, of varying caliber. Without military-grade munitions, good luck hitting a vulnerable point through a five-foot reinforced skull or a chest-cavity caged with ribs thicker than your leg.

Those stinging gunshot wounds *did* piss her off, though – five-tons of piss-off.

That nose didn't help either. It made hiding a practical impossibility. She simply followed your scent. Besides tall trees, Mark had spent the odd night tucked inside one mouse-hole or another while Rexy lounged outside, waiting, with slitted eyes.

Your only real option was to find places she couldn't go, like a rabbit aiming for the briar patch.

And with that, Mark abruptly jumped the old rusted guardrail and bolted for the trees.

There was an outraged roar as Rexy saw her long-pursued quarry evading her clutches once again. The trees were clustered close together, making it difficult for her to follow.

Not that she wouldn't try. Mark had stopped speculating what passed for a brain in the big rex, but this seemed personal.

It seemed personal when the animal continued to tail him after he'd left her territory, but they were in the mountains now. *T. rex* liked the lowlands. A creature from an era with a richer atmosphere, Rexy struggled in the higher altitudes. But she was still after him.

There was a heavy crash as Rexy broke past the guardrail and began to bludgeon her way through the trees.

The terrain was steep, and with the thin air, Mark was quickly winded as he circled back up towards the main road. If he could get Rexy tangled in the evergreens, he could put some distance between them.

*If.*

Trees toppled loudly behind him.

Mark jumped the guardrail, back onto the pavement, and began to run.

Another roar shook the branches as Rexy realized she'd been tricked.

Mark stretched out into a full sprint, dodging debris as he went. The road showed signs of deliberate clearance, but it was spotty, with plenty of loose branches and clumps of vegetation still blocking the way.

Behind him, Rexy stepped back onto the main road. Mark again felt the thunder of her footsteps as she broke into a run.

Mark spared a glance over his shoulder. It was going to be close.

They were moving sharply uphill. To his right was steep rock. With more distance, he might have tried scaling the cliff, but at this range, Rexy would be on him in moments.

His legs were already beginning to burn. The scattered clutter was working against him. He had to evade the bigger logs and branches, while Rexy simply powered-on through.

That was the rex-way, Mark thought grimly.

Up ahead was a patch of leaves – walking unoccupied, he might have simply tread through, but at full-stride, he instead took a hurdling leap, and cleared it.

Rexy, fast upon his heels, stepped firmly in the circle.

There was an elastic, reverberating *twang*, and the sound of heavy logs moving. Mark looked back and saw a rope encircle Rexy's foot, yanking her off her feet, upending her with a crash. Her outraged roar peaked into a shriek of pain.

Mark paused, watching breathless. Rexy was flipped onto her back, her foot dangling twelve-feet in the air. The rope-trap was clearly designed to catch something much smaller, but for simply tripping her up, it worked just fine.

A big animal like that was not designed to fall. Dare he hope she was injured?

But, no such luck. Rexy grunted painfully, but she was moving, legs starting to kick, already feeling for footing.

The wind was knocked out of her, though. She was moving slow.

That gave Mark a moment to root through his pack. He had found something that worked well against Rexy, provided he had time to use it.

Hiding didn't matter – that nose would ferret you right out. But now he had the opportunity to do something about that.

Time to plug up that nose.

From his bag, he pulled a tin of tear-gas, a safety item he'd taken to carrying with him. He popped the tin and the gas began to burn.

Rexy started to howl, already reacting to the familiar foul-burning stench, even before Mark threw it directly into her face.

Her response was an immediate, outraged bellow as the gas seared her eyes and sinuses, leaving her blinded and in agony.

She tended to work up a bit of temper-tantrum, too, so it was a maneuver best done with a little room to move. Mark turned and ran.

If he could get out of sight, that might be enough. With Rexy's nose temporarily neutralized, hiding was now possible. The old mountain road was a winding one, and if he could put some distance between them before she recovered, he was home safe.

A low, growling moan sounded behind him.

Rexy was stubborn, and this was not the first time she'd been gassed. She was fighting through it. Mark heard a wrenching sound as she yanked her foot free of the snare, bringing the tree down right along with it.

Mark ran for all he was worth. Around the next bend, he would duck back into the trees – this time uphill, into the higher rocks.

But as he rounded the corner, he was greeted by a startled scream.

A young woman, perhaps only a teenager, was standing in the middle of the road – he piled right into her, knocking them both to the ground.

For a moment, the two of them lay in a heap, staring at each other, wide-eyed.

Then Mark jumped up and grabbed her, throwing her over his shoulder and began to run.

The girl let out another scream and suddenly she was a whirling, clawed wildcat. Ignoring her scratching nails, Mark piled the two of them into the brush together, ducking under a low-hanging branch.

He pulled the girl close and dropped a hand over her mouth to stifle her screams, whereupon she immediately sank her teeth into his hand.

At that moment, Rexy rounded the corner, roaring madly, stamping her feet, clawing at her eyes.

The girl stiffened in his arms, sucking breath, her eyes growing wide.

"For God's sake," Mark whispered curtly, "shut up!"

He pulled them back into the brush out of sight.

Rexy padded down the path behind them.

Mark and the girl sat as silent as two frightened mice.

Rexy moved slowly, now. Mark suspected she knew he was close. But he could also see both her eyes and nose streaming mucus like tears.

She was in her stalking posture now. When she chose, the big tyrannosaur's stealth was remarkable. She must have weighed five-tons, but even this close, the reverberation in the ground from her footsteps had all but vanished.

But Mark could still hear her low moans – pain from her burning eyes – anger over losing her target once again.

Rexy's huge head and jaws passed directly overhead like the spotlight from a prison tower.

Mark pulled the girl closer – she was no longer struggling.

There was a long pause before Rexy turned away again. Mark hoped she didn't just simply curl up to lick her wounds, as she had done before. Several excruciating heartbeats passed as she scanned the bushes with watering, teary eyes.

Then she moved on down the road. Mark watched, breathless, until the big rex disappeared from sight.

She would be looking for him though.

# CHAPTER 3

Mark's hand had fallen away from the girl's mouth, but now he realized his arms remained latched tightly around her. He let go, stepping away, even as she jerked herself out of his grip.

She stared back at him warily.

"Hi," Mark ventured cautiously. "My name's Mark."

The girl said nothing. Mark held up his hands, non-threatening.

"Did you put out that trap?" he asked.

She nodded slowly.

"Well, it looks like I owe you one," Mark said, "Otherwise, she'd have caught me for sure."

The girl glanced down the path, where Rexy had disappeared, then looked back at Mark speculatively.

"That rex," she said. "It was *after* you, wasn't it?"

"Yeah, it was," Mark said, his smile fading.

He shut his eyes, helplessly reliving the last year-and-a-half all over again.

It was already a lifetime. The world that *was*, might as well have never existed.

Mark had gotten the very first look at the shape of things to come.

And while he might not have appreciated it at the time, that actually made him doubly fortunate, because that first look made him an *asset* – simply by virtue of being one of the first victims.

Mark suspected his own encounter was not the first time the Men in Black had heard of these odd pockets of what they insisted on calling *'mutants'* – after all, they had not let him go.

Or Sally.

The two of them had been housed together on one military base after another for more than a year – *'interned'*, not *'prisoners'* – just not free to come and go.

It was a lot *like* being a prisoner, just *not*. So, by definition, rights accorded prisoners did not apply.

Funny how words mattered.

The entire ordeal was hardest on Sally, who wasn't conditioned for roughing it, in jungles *or* protective custody, and the first four months of *that* were in Mexico.

Once back in the States, she was chronically ill, relapsing hardest when KT-day hit.

Mark and Sally watched it on TV, stationed on a base in Florida. They'd already seen the live-preview, but this was premier-night.

The new Mother Nature taking over.

In the weeks and months following KT-day, Sally continued to suffer recurring bouts of a malaria-style weakness, ever-ready to pounce back upon her. She was only just on the mend, finally regaining some healthy weight back, when she abruptly relapsed again, with a bout of severe nausea that had Mark worried.

It apparently concerned their keepers as well, because they finally decided to keep her in the infirmary overnight.

Naturally, it had to be *that* night.

The Apocalypse finally came down on them too.

Mark had, of course, *heard* of the Food of the Gods – everyone still alive had. He knew what it was, or at least what it *did.* He'd seen months of graphic video-footage as outbreaks bloomed all over the world.

But he'd never seen it in-person until that night.

He heard it coming hours away, like the rumble of an encroaching storm. Except this was in the ground, like an earthquake.

Then, somewhere in the dark hours of the night, it landed right on top of them.

Mark never saw it clearly. From his end, it was over fairly quickly – out of nowhere, the roof, and then his entire building tumbled down on top of him.

As he lay stunned, trapped under the rubble, he heard – *felt* – sounds – staccato tremors like the footsteps of some impossible giant, accompanied by reverberating bellows that might have echoed-up from the depths of a volcano.

The volcanic roars were quickly answered by munitions – bullets, bazookas, grenades, and rockets, all at once, all in succession – and Mark had seen enough video to already know it was all utterly useless.

Somewhere in the middle, a blast hit his building and knocked him unconscious.

When he awoke, the sounds of the giants had faded. There was nothing but dead, stony silence.

Coughing, choking dust, Mark dug his way free.

Climbing out from the pile of rubble, he had looked down on what was left of the base.

This was not a battle – the base was simply smashed flat.

Mark's eyes searched for the infirmary, where they had taken Sally, but it was impossible to even tell exactly where it had been.

Without realizing it, Mark started walking forward, his feet moving on their own. He might have called out Sally's name.

But then he stopped. There was nothing there – even the rubble was burning itself out.

Sally was gone.

Mark shut his eyes, forcing himself to accept that fact.

There was no moment of loneliness in his life comparable to it.

Then he heard the sound of choppers.

He stepped discreetly out of sight as they circled and landed near the center of the compound. Out came the spotlights, searching for survivors. Squads of soldiers fanned-out, spreading across the tarmac in quick formation.

Keeping to the shadows, Mark stole back along the fence to the edge of the forest.

Behind him, he heard boot-heels clapping concrete. Without a backward glance, he jumped the fence and ducked quickly into the trees.

Mark knew he was leaving all that was left of civilization behind, venturing alone out into whatever world waited.

He met Rexy the very next day.

# CHAPTER 4

"How long has that rex been after you?" the girl asked. The wariness in her eyes had perked into speculative interest.

Mark shrugged, tossing up a count on his fingers.

"About six weeks now," he said.

The girl raised her brows.

"You must be hard to catch."

"So far," Mark replied, holding up crossed fingers.

She continued to stare. Her intense scrutiny was actually starting to make him nervous.

He glanced around the surrounding brush – pretty young things like this were sometimes used as lures – the old coyote-ploy.

"So," Mark ventured, "what's your name?"

Her head cocked, mistrustful as a deer who had never seen a person before – curious but skittish, ready to bolt.

"I'm Lily," she said, finally. "My name's Lily."

Mark smiled.

"Nice to meet you, Lily."

He reached to shake her hand formally, but she held back, her eyes on him like a cat. Mark lowered his hand.

"Do you live around here?" he asked.

Lily nodded.

"Just you?" Mark prodded gently.

She shook her head.

"No. Me and my sisters. We've been here a few months now."

"How many are you?" Mark asked, leaning forward – prompting a quick fade from the skittish deer. Mark raised his hands.

"Sorry. I don't mean to scare you. I'm just passing through."

Lily's dark eyes blinked.

"Where are you headed?" she asked.

Mark gave her another tired smile.

"Home," he said.

Lily regarded him closely, eyes narrowed.

Then she stepped forward and grabbed him by the hand.

"Come back with me," she said, and suddenly her eyes were those of an eager teenager. "We have food. You can sleep there."

She pulled his hand, pointing down the path.

Mark stumbled hesitantly into step.

"Uh, really… I don't want to be any trouble."

But Lily tugged him along.

"No. Please, come. My sisters will want to meet you."

Now she smiled.

"They'll want to hear about the rex."

With a touch of trepidation, Mark allowed himself to be led deeper into the forest.

They did not make it far, however, before the drone of rotor-blades sounded in the distance. After a few minutes, a military helicopter came into view.

One thing about the new world, even things that were once familiar, now seemed threatening. The chopper's motor roared, suddenly loud and close, as it zoomed overhead like a hunting hawk.

Mark stepped back into the trees, pulling Lily with him. This time she drew close to him, actually clinging to him, her eyes wide.

Lily stared after the flying machine as if with superstitious dread. It might as well have been a pterodactyl or a giant croc – they had both of them out there these days.

Mark guessed Lily was around eighteen. She wouldn't have been raised a cave-girl. What was she before? A high school kid? She wasn't some primitive who didn't know what a helicopter was.

That woodsy-wild look in her eyes made Mark nervous. People got weird in isolated groups, and survival situations removed the trappings of civilization very quickly – *everybody* was crazy these days.

A week before, he'd passed a couple on the road who told him the world had been taken over by demons, and it was all just a regular, old-fashioned, abominations-from-the-pit sort of Apocalypse.

To be fair, Mark, with only inklings of the truth himself, didn't really have a much better story to tell.

His own version was scuttlebutt off the military bases. Genetic engineering out of control. An urban-legend-thing. Instead of Area 51, it was 'Monster Island'.

Still – it *looked* like abominations-from-the-pit.

That soothsaying couple had frowned when Mark told them he was headed for the mountains. The woman tried to warn him off – something about 'dark spirits'.

Whatever *that* meant. Neither of them would elaborate, and Mark had left them on their way.

He did find himself quietly amused that, in a world like *this*, he would scoff at the supernatural.

On the other hand, it *was* a warning he did not take lightly. Supernatural or not, Mark knew there were all kinds of things running around, that could easily pass for evil spirits or demons.

Of course, he had gone up the mountain anyway. Ignoring the harbinger, he went right on ahead with the trespass – the first transgression. Thus, he could be appropriately punished.

He had already been nearly eaten. Now, another kind of predator circled overhead, as a second and then a third chopper came into view.

Lily trembled as one of the birds banked directly above. For a moment, Mark thought they had been spotted.

Then the chopper continued on. After a few minutes, a dozen more appeared, and passed by, following the first – an entire squadron.

"There's been a lot of them lately," Lily said, furtively.

Mark glanced down at her wide-eyes.

A *lot* of them?

Clearly, Lily didn't like that.

When the last chopper faded in the distance, Lily grabbed his hand again, pulling him back out onto the path.

"Come on," she said, and then she turned and ran on ahead.

*Coyote-ploy*, Mark thought again, as he fell into step behind her.

The terrain maintained a steady incline, and as they went, more of the road was cleared away, although not enough for vehicle traffic, staying narrow, and entwining through the overgrowth. Anything wider than a mountain bike couldn't make it through.

Lily flounced lightly ahead, while Mark followed at a huffing lope. Then she broke off the path where a dead-fall of fallen trees blocked the road.

Just beyond, the land leveled off into a clearing, and Mark realized they stood at the edge of a good-sized river. It split the cliff, which was outfitted with a modest dam.

The facility appeared operational and functioning.

Although, Mark noted the road running alongside had crumbled away, leaving nothing but the cliff and the dam itself on their side of the river.

It rather resembled a medieval fortress – a guard-wall with a moat.

Lily was running ahead of him.

“Come on!” she shouted, waving.

“How far?” Mark shouted back.

Lily smiled broadly.

“We’re already here!”

She was following a footpath along the water’s edge. Mark trailed behind her, slipping on rocks that were damp and slick with river spray.

As they drew closer, Mark realized the road above was not just a through-way across the river, but a station for an old sawmill.

The saw-yard was outfitted with a large crane that looked as if it had seen recent use, probably re-purposed to bring supplies up from the basin floor.

It was actually a fairly modern set-up. Someone simply turned the facility on, and outfitted the entire area with hydro-power.

At the base of the dam was an elevator. The open-shaft was empty and Mark could see the carrier-cage parked at the top.

Lily pushed a large red button – a buzzer sounded and the cage began to descend.

Mark could hear the click of rusted pins and the whine of old cables. He wondered how long this contraption had been there – how many seasons, carrying tons and more, up there winter after winter?

There was a loud screech as the elevator ground to a stop. Lily pulled the bar open and beckoned him inside. She was smiling openly, her furtive spookiness completely gone.

Mark looked up top, wondering who was up there waiting.

With an imperceptible groan, he stepped into the cage.

The cables screeched again, followed by an abrupt lurch as the cage cranked back up. Mark counted seconds until they reached the top.

This time the back of the cage slid open, and Mark got his first good look at where Lily lived.

The dam doubled as a bridge where the road crossed over the river. It rejoined the hillside at the edge of a wide, paved clearing – the saw-yard, backed by the mill itself, and then, what looked like office buildings.

Beyond the lot, the foliage had grown heavy, but it was manicured crisply around the site itself, creating a deliberately artistic, hedged appearance.

As yet, there was still no sign of any other living person.

Lily pulled Mark's hand and he followed her out into the open.

On cue, there was a flash of movement from the shadows and the surrounding brush. Within seconds, Mark was surrounded and found himself staring at a circle of wooden spears.

He blinked, raising his hands, looking around at his assailants.

They were all women.

Their garb was the ragged-remains of California beachwear, out of place in the mountains, except for the adaptation of sticks and leaves braided into their uniformly long hair. Once, the style would have been called *'Earthy'*.

Here, it was more evocative of some savage, primitive tribe.

Their eyes were wild. Their spear-tips were sharp and none too shy, pressing into his back and neck.

The young woman in front, tall and lithe like a gymnast, stepped forward purposefully, raising her spear.

But Lily interceded.

"Michelle, wait! He's not one of them."

Michelle glanced sideways at Lily, not lowering her spear, bringing the tip up to Mark's throat.

"He saved me," Lily insisted. "We were chased by a rex."

Michelle's ears perked.

"That big female that's been hanging around?"

"It's after *him*," Lily said, nodding.

Michelle's eyes narrowed at Mark. With some reluctance, she lowered her spear.

"Chased by a rex," Michelle said. "Yeah, we've seen *that* before. That's how we ended up here."

Mark said nothing, standing with his hands still dutifully raised. But Michelle and the rest of the cadre stepped back, lowering their spears.

Lily pulled Mark's raised hands down to his side.

Michelle eyed Mark balefully.

Then she turned, looking up to the sky after the chopper squadron. She regarded Lily.

"Did they see you?"

Lily shook her head, and there was relieved murmur as her superstitious reaction seemed mirrored in the others.

Michelle measured Mark with a long stare, her hand tightening compulsively on her spear.

But then she turned and began walking back towards the mill. The others fanned-out behind Mark, corralling him. He saw the young woman to his right also packed a pistol on her hip.

The saw-yard gave way to the first office building, and just beyond, Mark realized there were on-site employee living quarters. All very modern – electric lights and everything. But the no-frills, rustic-industrial structure had been domesticated, decorated with that earthy-granola touch.

Michelle fell into step beside him. Mark risked a tentative smile.

"Nice set-up you've got here," he offered.

Michelle's glare never wavered.

"Those choppers," Mark asked. "Lily said they've been around lately?"

Michelle eyed him suspiciously. His garb was civilian, but military issue.

"Yes, they have," she said finally. "And we usually try to avoid contact with outsiders."

With that, she put her fingers to her lips and let loose a startlingly loud whistle. The apparently empty saw-yard suddenly buzzed alive like a beehive.

Now there were dozens of eyes on him, surrounding him, all blinking with that same mistrustful scrutiny.

Again – they were all women.

Lily said she lived with her 'sisters', but this was obviously not a literal family colony – there was no kin-resemblance among them.

Yet, there *was* uniformity – they were all muscled like dancers, with long manes of hair, surprisingly well-kept, with a simple dress of cut-offs and earth-tones, that blended invisibly with the foliage.

"You have no men here?" Mark asked.

Michelle turned a sour eye.

"*No*," she said, coldly.

"But we *used* to," another voice chimed in.

A short, compact woman, a bit older than the rest, but still whip-chorded like a surfer-girl, stepped forward to meet them. She regarded Mark appraisingly.

"I'm Ginger," she said. "What's your story? AWOL?"

"He was being chased by a rex," Lily said, like a girl showing-off a new puppy.

Ginger's brows raised.

"That big female," she said, nodding. "She's a sour-tempered one. She's been hanging around for the last couple weeks."

Mark blinked. "Really? A couple of weeks?"

Rexy must have actually beaten him into the mountains.

"Yes," Michelle replied, eyeing Mark. "And now we know she's here because of *you*."

Ginger patted Michelle's spear-hand patiently, preferring to hear Mark's story before stabbing him.

"So…," Ginger said. "This rex? Why is it after you?"

Mark cleared his voice.

"I… sort of stumbled into its nest."

Ginger nodded.

"A mother's rage," she said.

Mark glanced uncomfortably at Michelle's spear.

"I've never seen an animal that obsessive," he said.

"*T. rex* are like that," Ginger replied.

"Yeah," Lily said. "Something like that happened where we came from."

Ginger and Michelle both flashed dark eyes in Lily's direction. Lily fell immediately silent.

She did not, however, let go of Mark's hand.

Mark was feeling those familiar prickly hairs on the back of his neck.

"Y'know," he said, starting to pull away from Lily's grip, "I'm really only passing through. I'm getting a strong feeling that I'm not wanted here, so perhaps it's better if I just be on my way."

But Lily's grip clenched and she pulled back, glaring at the others with a teenager's temper.

"No, wait, it's alright! Michelle's just being protective. Please stay. We have food."

Mark looked around – push came to shove, they still had a lot of spears.

Michelle's face darkened at Lily's outburst, while Ginger's lips turned up in an amused grin.

But it was Michelle who finally nodded.

"Alright," she said. "You're welcome to stay the night."

Mark almost snickered – Michelle's voice carried all the invitation of a rattling snake, and her aggressive, unwavering eyes were more predatory than protective.

The hairs on his neck advised giving anyone with eyes like *that* immediate distance.

Of course, there *were* even more base instincts – Lily had also said, *'food'*.

Sometimes the simplest lures are what spring us. Mark had lost twenty pounds on the road – six weeks living out of scavenged cans and packages, left-overs from the old-world, along with the occasional critter or bird roasted over a fire.

Lily smiled up at him.

Michelle's frown remained. As did Ginger's small smirk.

Welcome to my parlor, Mark thought, and allowed himself to be led on.

# CHAPTER 5

"Okay," Ginger said, as they sat down to dinner, "tell us why you're here, and why you're on the run from the military."

Mark looked around the table uncomfortably, but the smell of hot food held him in place – after a year-and-a-half of military cuisine, a home-style meal with all the trimmings was like a trip back in time.

Lily and her sisters made full-use of what might as well have been a survivalist-storage camp. Logger's barracks took on the ambiance of a roadside inn. The cafeteria was a fully-fitted kitchen with a dining-hall, and a storage-locker stocked with supplies. They even managed to salvage most of the frozen goods, sealed in lockers in the frigid mountains.

The dining-hall was lit and heated by the central fireplace, where the chimney split the building from the living quarters. A stack of logs lined either side.

They tended to just keep the fire going, Ginger explained – no sense using precious electricity when the old ways worked just as well – it heated both the water and the building.

Once the sun set, the rustic dining-room was cast in flickering firelight, like an old-time drinking hall.

Like *Beowulf*, where the monster, Grendel, took prey in terrifying nighttime raids.

The tables were lit by candlelight, and the dress-tone of his hosts now seemed more Goth than earthy.

Mark was seated opposite Michelle and Ginger, along with several of the women who had escorted him from the saw-yard.

On his right was Luna – like Ginger, older than the rest, with a soulful, elegantly beautiful face, the supple limbs of a dancer, and *ancient* eyes.

Of all his hosts, she seemed the most demure.

She had also pressed her spear hardest against his back.

Mark noticed a scar running down the left side of her face. He wondered if a man had done that.

At Luna's right was Serena, not much older than Lily, who gawked at Mark with the same feral fascination, as if she'd never seen a man before.

Christine was the one with the gun on her hip. She stayed mostly silent, but her furtive glances were even less welcoming than Michelle's Doberman-stare.

Lily sat to Mark's left, pertly proper – pleased to be at the grown-up table – evidently, an honor afforded as his escort. Her face was like a kid who'd found a stray dog – *can I keep him?*

The rest of the dining-hall remained subdued. A low murmur of hushed voices circulated, as heads from other tables bobbed towards their table.

"Well?" Ginger prodded. "What's your story? Are you military?"

Mark shook his head.

"I was interned. That's actually how I survived KT-day." He shrugged. "I was sort of an early witness, and they thought that might be valuable. But after a while it was keeping us in custody, just because we were in custody."

"*We?*" Ginger's eyes perked.

Mark shifted uncomfortably in his seat.

"I was interned with someone," he said. "She died."

"*She?*" Ginger nodded. "What was her name?"

Mark eyed the circle around him, and felt judgment hanging over his every word.

"Her name was Sally," he said. "And yes, she was important to me."

"What happened to her?"

Mark shrugged.

"Our base got hit by infected-giants. Just like the rest of the world. What can I say? I made it out. She didn't."

He eyed his hosts directly.

"It's actually still kind of fresh," he said. "If you don't mind, I'd rather not talk about it."

"Alright," Ginger said agreeably, leaning back in her chair. "Then how about you tell us about the *T. rex*?"

Now, the room went silent. When Mark glanced over his shoulder, every eye in the place was on him.

"Why," Ginger asked, "is there a female rex after you?"

"That," Mark said, "is another one I'd rather not talk about."

Ginger eyed him fixedly. Michelle stared unblinking.

Mark sighed.

"It was the day after I escaped the base," he said. "I walked into her nest."

There was a murmur from the tables around him – a jury hearing confession, ready to render judgment.

Fair enough. It wasn't like there was any part of it Mark was proud of.

The hell of it was, he and Sally were already planning to escape on their own. They had been quietly gathering supplies, including a pilfered pistol and ammo. But Sally had fallen sick.

Mark would spend long hours agonizing in the following weeks, wondering if there was anything different he could have done.

Once he'd hopped the fence that night, he had run, blindly, headlong through the trees, knowing perfectly well he was running as much as anything from Sally, and the reality that he finally failed her – so he just kept going, heedless of the slap and slash of branches and leaves.

He finally hit the point of exhaustion, right around the blink of twilight, just as the first streaks of dawn filtered through the trees. His adrenaline spent, Mark simply collapsed beside an overgrown log, pulled his jacket around him, and fell into a fitful sleep.

When he awoke, it was still early morning. Damp with dew, Mark shivered in the chilly air. When he tried to move, he discovered his bones and tendons were stiff and sprung. He'd been inactive too long and his conditioning showed it.

He pulled out his pack, going over the provisions he'd stocked over previous weeks. And it was just serendipitous that he happened to be loading the stolen service pistol, when he stumbled into the rex-nest.

Mark had, of course, seen *T. rex* hatchlings before, no bigger than turkeys – he'd watched them eat a grown man alive.

This brood was larger than that. Mark counted eight, each the size of a Great Dane, probably yearlings – long and gangly-limbed, just starting into that early stage of rapid growth.

When he stumbled into the clearing, it was like triggering a strand on a spider-web – a crack of a branch, the clip of a twig, and they all came running, jaws agape.

Mark snapped the cartridge into the pistol, drew a bead and fired.

The first of the little dragons snapped-up straight, as if to attention, before falling limp. The sharp retort momentarily spooked the others, and Mark was able to take out two more while they hesitated.

But then they all swarmed him at once.

One thing about *T. rex* – they came at you headfirst, and that gave you a target. Of course, with a grown rex, that meant five-feet of reinforced skull. But these yearlings were much more fragile.

His back up against heavy brush, Mark had no choice but to simply pick his targets one after the other.

The little handgun wasn't what he'd had in mind for defense against the wildlife – it was mostly intended to get him off the base. He'd planned on finding something higher-caliber once he was on the road.

But for these smaller beasts, it was sufficient.

In a few short seconds, it was over. Mark emptied the clip as the last of the yearlings collapsed barely a yard from his foot.

There was a beat of silence as the echo of gunshots faded.

Then, approaching from the woods, came the heavy grunt of something *big*.

Looking around at the despoiled nest, Mark turned quickly back the way he'd come.

He had been walking downhill when he stumbled into the nest, and the path back was steep and slippery. There was a terrible dream-like moment where his feet seemed to slide uselessly in the mud, before he caught his traction and pulled himself up into the thick shrubbery surrounding the clearing.

There was surer footing in the trees beyond, and Mark spared one glance over his shoulder.

That was when he had gotten his first look at her.

She hadn't spotted him yet – her attention was rooted on her pillaged nest. Mark heard a low, almost human-like moan as the big rex crouched over her dead children.

There was something deceptive about seeing a *T. rex* up close – it was like watching a moose after being around deer. The same movements seemed cumbersome on the larger scale, but they were not slow.

And when it moved, it moved with *power*.

Standing over the bodies of her dead yearlings, Rexy threw back her head and *roared*.

A foghorn – a mother's rage given form.

And then, in that same, false slow-motion movement, she turned and looked right at Mark through the trees.

That was the first time she saw *him*.

Mark turned and ran.

He had pretty much been running ever since.

# CHAPTER 6

“A mother's rage,” Ginger repeated, as Mark finished his story.

She glanced to the others, who nodded back.

“You asked about our men," Ginger said, eyeing Mark meaningfully. “They died.”

He already suspected that much. Now he sat to attention.

Behind him, the dining-hall also sat in rapt silence.

“It's been six months,” Ginger said.

Mark looked around the table. Michelle's glare was unwavering. And while Luna’s face remained serene, Mark could see that scar on her cheek darken as if with clenching teeth. Christine stayed silent, her hands out of sight, perhaps fingering the holster of her pistol.

Lily blinked, wide-eyed, around at her elders.

“They were real men’s men,” Ginger continued, smiling ruefully. “They took to survivalism right away.” She chuckled. “They called themselves the ‘wolf-pack’.

A small titter echoed briefly across the room.

“And what happened to them?” Mark asked.

This time it was Michelle who answered, and there was no hint of a smile in *her* face.

“They pissed-off a *rex*-pack,” she said.

The background titter was immediately doused. Mark looked around the room at the haunted eyes staring back.

*Six months.* Fresh trauma.

"They raided a nest," Michelle continued. "They were hunter/gatherers. Providing for the women-folk. They became plunderers."

Christine and Luna both nodded reproachfully.

"They'd been on a week-long hunt," Ginger explained. "They stumbled on fresh hatchlings. A gaggle of turkeys with teeth, they said. And they killed them all. Grabbed up the eggs too."

Mark shut his eyes. He *knew* what came next.

"The adults followed them home," he said.

"They came right into camp that night," Ginger replied.

Mark shut his eyes. He didn't *have* to imagine.

He could see them now – the whole pack of them, stalking you in the dark, padding with that impossible stealth, until they were right on top of you.

Mark understood his hosts a little better now.

*That* was why they lived at the top of a hundred-foot fortress – no one was sneaking up on them again.

"How did *you* escape?" Mark asked.

Ginger shrugged.

"We stayed out of the way," she said. "It wasn't *us* they were after."

Mark nodded. He could testify personally that tyrannosaurs had a tendency to focus their aggression.

"They *got* who they were after," Michelle said, eyeing Mark meaningfully. "Sooner or later, they always do."

Mark nodded, understanding.

"I'm a danger to you," he said.

He stood from the table.

"I guess that means I should leave."

That brought instant protest from Lily, who grabbed his hand, standing with him.

"No, wait! Don't go!"

She turned imploringly to Michelle and Ginger.

"We can't just let him leave. It's dark out."

Michelle appeared unmoved. Christine and Luna sat implacably.

But Ginger waved Lily down placatingly.

"Relax, child," she said, "we aren't going to turn him out into the night. He *did* save your life, after all."

Beside him, Lily squeezed Mark's hand.

"Although," Ginger added, turning to Mark, "it was *you* that put her in danger in the first place."

"Understood," Mark said.

Ginger nodded. She turned to Lily.

"You can set him up in one of the empty rooms."

Lily practically bounced, tugging Mark's hand.

Mark followed dutifully, noting how their council of elders seemed to have passed him off to Lily's care. They obviously recognized Lily's attentions and apparently decided to indulge her.

Or perhaps it was as simple as '*you found him, you take care of him.*'

There was also the possibility he was being fattened-up like a cow.

People got weird in small groups.

The looks he was getting from the other girls weren't comforting – the same unabashed, teenage eagerness, especially Serena, who earned herself a jealous sideways scowl from Lily.

He reminded himself of what these girls had been through and tried to be understanding.

That did not mean *trusting*.

As Lily led him out of the dining-hall onto the grounds, she grabbed-up a bucket of scraps, taking them around back, beckoning Mark to follow. In the darkness behind the dining-hall was a large doghouse.

Lily smiled widely.

"You haven't met Junior," she said, holding up the bucket.

There was a squawk from the doghouse and a flash of teeth, clamping shut with a gator-like *snap*.

Lily laughed as Mark jumped back. But the snapping jaws only reached out a couple of feet, and as he looked closer, Mark saw why.

It was a rex-hatchling, curled up in a blanket. It had a broken leg, set in a cast.

The little dragon stared up at Mark balefully. Then it bleated, and Lily began feeding it the scraps.

*Ohhhh, boy*, Mark thought, *that is* such *a bad idea.*

To Mark's utter astonishment, Lily actually kneeled right down beside the baby rex, as it snapped the scraps out of her hand, kissing at it like a puppy.

"We found him alone in the woods," Lily said. "With a broken leg, he would have died for sure."

Mark wondered if it was a woman-thing. He'd known girls who lived alone, no boyfriend, but with a dog the size of a Mack truck – pit-bulls, Rottweilers – basically, a canine version of a sawed-off shotgun.

Rather than the gun, they seemed to trust a powerful animal, even a dangerous one, that could potentially overpower them.

Lily smiled at his expression.

"Joshua," she said, "didn't like the rex much either. The only good rex was a dead one." Lily frowned, looking at Mark curiously. "Why do men always want to *kill* an animal?"

Lily scratched the baby rex behind the ears. It thumped its leg reflexively.

"We just want to… make friends."

And *there*, Mark thought, was the appeal of the pit-bull over the shotgun – it was something she could befriend, that she could feed and care for, which would, in turn, look after her personally.

Bonding was not the end-goal – just the control-mechanism.

The purpose was to harness this creature's power through empathy, understanding its wants, its moods, instincts – learning how you could make it behave simply by touching it in different ways. It was the heart of domestication and inherent in the nesting instinct.

Mark watched as Lily fawned over the little rex, who seemed content allowing itself to be petted.

The little creature was remarkably doglike. It reminded Mark of a monitor lizard he had seen once – a pet that responded to its keeper the same way.

What did he really *know* about *T. rex*? They were bird-relatives – something he never really appreciated until he saw one alive. They were not feathered like speculative drawings he'd seen, but they did have hair-like quills, reminiscent of the scarce hairs on an elephant's hide.

The bird-heritage was in their posture, their movement – how surprisingly light they were on their feet.

He also knew birds were literally smart enough to talk, at least enough to ask for crackers.

If a monitor was capable of such doglike behavior, and a parrot knew enough to ask for food, what about a rex?

Lily tapped the hatchling on the cheek and it sat up pertly, waiting for the command.

"Catch!" she said, tossing another scrap. 'Junior' snapped the morsel out of the air, cocking its head, looking for more.

"See?" Lily said. "They learn."

She petted the little rex, who now settled down, leaning its chin on her leg, making a cooing sound, oddly like a purr.

So this was a pet, Mark thought, and *he* was a self-confessed nest-plunderer.

The little rex eyed him suspiciously.

As if it *knew*.

Mark had never told that story to anyone before today. He never had the occasion to.

He actually felt bad about the whole thing. It wasn't like he questioned *why* that big mama-rex hated him. Rexy's point of view was simple – he killed her children.

As Lily stroked her pet baby rex, Mark now found himself wondering exactly where this hatchling had come from.

Rexy had apparently beaten him to the mountains. As Lily's sisters told it, she'd been around a couple weeks. And he had encountered her on the way *up* the hill.

The nest he had inadvertently plundered was yearlings. Had Rexy been getting ready for another brood? Was that what she had been doing the last couple of weeks in the mountains?

That might explain why she hadn't come after him until now.

It would also mean…

Mark groaned, looking down at Junior.

Unless there was another adult female *T. rex* running around the steep terrain of the Colorado Rockies, this was Rexy's hatchling.

Mark glanced back in the direction of the dam.

He didn't *think* that big rex could get up here.

But between *his* presence and her own hatchling, combined with that damned bloodhound nose of hers, it simply wasn't possible she wouldn't *try*.

Lily tossed Junior the last of the scraps, wiping her hands on her cut-offs. Junior squawked, but Lily patted his head and shushed him back into his little house.

Then she took Mark's hand again.

"Come along," she said. "Let me show you your room."

Mark hesitated.

As he had watched this young girl/woman fawn over a tiny dragon, he was actually a bit touched.

After everything she'd been through, she found solace extending compassion to a small, injured animal.

And specifically an infant of the very animal that hurt her.

Touching. But telling.

It was like a person bitten by a snake, who then develops a deep interest, even collecting and working with them. It was a way of beating fear, as if making friends would stop the snake from biting you.

As Lily led him across the compound, Mark found himself feeling a little sorry for her.

He thought again about Rexy prowling somewhere in the hillside below.

On short acquaintance, despite her freaky-sisters, he liked this girl. He didn't want anything to happen to her just because she offered him shelter for the night.

Although, it appeared Lily was leading him away from the living quarters, back towards the office building. Apparently, he wasn't going to be bunking in the girl's dorm.

Lily lit an oil lantern and handed it over for Mark to carry as she opened the glass security door.

"The lights work, but we don't overuse the juice," she said.

She led him inside and upstairs. The lower-floors had been adapted for storage, while the upper-floor looked like a rec-area – a game and exercise room, with a large TV.

Lily brought Mark to what had once been the on-site exec's room, dominated by a large desk and a couch.

Last guy on Earth, Mark thought dryly, in a colony of women, and he was sleeping on the couch.

Although, as Lily brought his blankets and pillows, he suspected she might have other ideas.

She looked at least eighteen – not that much younger than he was.

Lily stood at the door, her dark eyes blinking.

“Do you need anything?” she asked.

Mark tossed his blanket and pillow over his shoulder.

“I think I’m fine.”

Lily hesitated, clearly hanging on an invitation. But Mark leaned resolutely against the door, smiling neutrally.

“Goodnight, Lily,” he said.

“Okay,” she said, a bit nonplussed, “Goodnight.”

She rose on her toes and kissed his cheek.

Then she disappeared down the hall.

Mark looked out the window, and saw her heading back across the grounds.

He settled down on the couch – surprisingly comfortable – but there was absolutely no chance he would sleep.

Something was not right here.

He supposed it was natural enough to be on edge. Rexy damn near caught him today. And now military choppers were flying around. The last thing he wanted was contact with the military.

Six months ago, that might have meant being taken into ‘protective custody’ – a blanket policy assigned to all unauthorized civilians, i.e. ‘refugees’, found wandering near bases.

But things had changed. Already an indentured guest, Mark heard the rumors.

After KT-day, surviving military sites experienced an exodus – stragglers congregated from miles around, looking for food, lodging, medicine – basically looking to be taken care of – and it wasn't long before quotas were maxed.

Mark hadn't seen a lot of trouble on his own base, overseen by General Rhodes himself. There was just one incident, which Mark did not actually witness, involving a small group of survivors who appeared on their front gate – three men and three women.

Mark wasn't there, but he *had* heard bullets.

Most versions of the story maintained the civilians shot first.

Mark didn't care – he had done his time with the military, and if Rhodes' people had found their way to the mountains, he had no intention of staying.

The chopper that buzzed past yesterday was close enough to spot them. Mark didn't *think* they did, or he would have expected at least a second fly-by, but it was too close anyway.

Throw in Rexy prowling about, and this fortress on the mountain felt more like propped-up bait.

But it was that baby rex that finally got him moving.

Not just for it being there, not even that it was very likely Rexy's own chick, *or* the fact that it was damnable foolishness to keep it in the compound.

It was the way it looked at him. Like it *knew*.

And so, as ungrateful as it might be to his hostesses, Mark was in the wind.

Around midnight, he let himself out into the yard, his pack over his shoulder.

# CHAPTER 7

The compound was dead silent. Keeping to the shadows, Mark trailed the fence until he spotted the night sentries. He wanted no spears in his face.

He made his way to the back of the compound, opposite the dam. The road, broken and blocked behind him, *should* continue on into the hills.

However, the path leading out of the mill appeared open and ungated – which seemed highly unlikely. The area was also generally dark, with no torchlight.

He saw only one lone watchman – Serena had pulled night-duty. But her beat-path seemed focused on safeguarding the dormitory, rather than policing the rear grounds.

Mark frowned indecisively. They had four guards posted along the dam, over a hundred-feet of sheer wall, but not here. That might not bode well for thc accessibility of the roadway up the hill.

He waited until Serena's rounds took her around the corner, and briefly out of sight, before he slipped back out to the old logging road.

Mark did not see the shadow separate from the dormitory, falling into step behind him, but it wasn't long before he became aware he was being followed.

All that time on the road with a five-ton *T. rex* prowling on his heels – a deceptively *stealthy* rex –

had left him remarkably attuned to the odd shuffling in the woods.

Particularly at night.

Mark picked up his pace.

But he was only a quarter mile past the gate, when he discovered why security in this direction was minimal.

They had apparently blown-up the canyon wall. What was once road was now a mound of boulders and debris.

Mark sighed, resigned. With no way around it, and feeling uncomfortably exposed under the open moonlight, he began picking his way around and over the rocks.

He was halfway over, when he heard a kick of rock behind him.

Mark paused stone-still, listening.

Someone was following him through the dead-fall.

Mark jumped down off the rocks to the other side. The road beyond was unmaintained gravel. Conscious of his footsteps, he stepped quickly into the bushes and waited.

He heard another scrape of falling rock and now a shadow appeared on the road.

When it passed his tree, Mark pounced, grabbing the slight figure bodily in his arms.

Quick as a cat, he clapped his hand over Lily's mouth to silence her startled scream.

“Damn it, Lily! What the hell are you doing?”

Mark released her, pushing her away roughly.

“Why are you following me?”

Lily looked up at him, pleading.

"I don't want you to leave."

"You heard your friends," Mark said. "I'm dangerous to have around."

"You don't have to leave tonight," Lily protested. "Stay just a little while."

"Lily," Mark said sternly, "you have to go home."

But she grabbed his hand, pulling at him as she had before.

"At least let me show you the way down the mountain."

Mark dug his feet.

"*No*," he said, pulling her hand loose.

Lily stared back at him, starting to look tearful.

"I'll follow you," she said stubbornly.

"And I'll tie you to a tree, if I have to," Mark said. He shook his head. "Go home, Lily."

He turned and began to walk, a deliberate march, leaving her behind. He waited for her footfalls on the gravel, but none came. He glanced back and saw her perched indecisively, a silhouette in the mist.

Then, as the moonlight faded behind a cloud, he lost sight of her.

The next moment, he was blinded from above.

There was a hawk-like roar, and Mark felt a blast of wind as a chopper zoomed in low. Without thought, he threw himself into the bushes.

The first chopper was immediately joined by a second. Their spotlights were out, spearing the darkness, circling the clearing just past the dead-fall.

In their spotlights, running for the rocks, was Lily.

Both choppers were on the ground in moments, and Mark could hear indistinct commands barked over the loudspeakers.

He also heard Lily's outraged screams as a handful of troops pulled her out of the rocks, fighting all the way.

Mark's breath let out in a low whisper.

"*Damn it.*"

Both choppers' motors sputtered to a stop, and troops fanned out on both sides.

Mark heard conversation – a soldier's voice.

"No, sir, it's not her."

There was a crackle of indistinct radio-static.

"A young woman," the soldier answered.

There was more static. The commanding officer waved his hand, and the spotlights turned out into the surrounding woods.

Mark faded back into the trees.

Lily was pulled aboard the first chopper.

The ground-troops scouted the area. So far, their attention was focused on the dead-fall, where Lily had been trying to escape – clearly a deliberate blockade.

That meant they would probably explore further.

Mark watched them peruse the perimeter, and knew it would not be long before they rooted him out.

But then, for some reason, they apparently decided not to pursue the matter tonight. Mark heard more indistinct bursts of radio-static, and the commander ordered his troops back.

In moments, both choppers were back in the air. The lights flared past like UFOs as they disappeared over the trees.

With Lily.

*Damn,* Mark thought.

*Dammit, dammit, dammit.*

He *so* much wished he could just turn and walk away.

The thought of Sally, of course, wouldn't let him.

"*Dammit,*" Mark said aloud, as he turned, following the choppers back down the mountain.

# CHAPTER 8

Little did Mark know, when that chopper had buzzed them yesterday, someone *had* indeed seen them. But this witness kept silent – a painful lesson she had learned well.

And ironically, while she had not been close enough to actually recognize Mark, she automatically flashed to the last time she'd seen him.

Sally Crawford looked back down at the forest floor. She had just gotten a brief glimpse of two people huddled in the trees, a man and a woman, before the chopper flew past.

The pilot, a rugged-looking guy everyone called Cap, stared straight ahead, missing the movement below. Both privates, Weaver and Emmett, her '*guards*', dozed in their seats.

There was no good reason to call out the two people on the ground. The last thing the surviving military forces wanted was refugees.

As one of those favored few, Sally was learning a whole new perspective on scarce resources.

Before KT-day, she was raised in *polite* society. She only recently left home, living away at college, amused at the quaintly meager furnishings of her rented apartment, but always aware that she *really* came from better circumstances.

Then the wreck of the *Pacific Princess* happened, and a two-week tropical cruise between terms became a preview for the end of the world.

No one died until they made it ashore.

Then *everyone* died. Including her father. Including the high-society young man who had parleyed with her father for her hand.

Sally would have died too, if not for a young crew-member she'd only just met.

Mark Bakker reminded Sally of a lot of spring flings, on a lot of vacations growing-up – Mark was the local boy at the beach-town.

Except *this* vacation-fling saved her life – first, the night the ship went down, and then…

Well, then, in all the days after.

Before *those* days, Sally's version of '*roughing it*' meant sharing a room in some posh sorority or campus apartment. It sounded so silly to her now, snobbish even – the idea that she was only 'slumming it' out in the world.

Or with a guy like Mark Bakker – the one that had gotten her out alive.

In the jungle, Sally had clung to him like a child. And in the months after, once they finally returned to the States, she was afraid to let him out of her sight.

But eventually Mark had been taken from her too. Six weeks ago, now.

She'd been sick for months, but they had to pick *that* day to finally bring her to the infirmary – the one night they'd been apart in over a year.

Sally smiled, a little bittersweet – the nurse had to practically throw Mark out after he sat at her bedside all day. She remembered how he squeezed her hand, as he was being pulled away.

"Keep a candle burning for me," he said.

Those were the last words he ever spoke to her.

That was the night the Apocalypse previewed on that beach finally caught up with them.

Sally actually didn't remember anything at all. The nurse had given her a mild sedative. The next thing she knew was waking-up in the dark among the rubble of the infirmary.

In the groggy aftermath, she sat up, coughing dust.

Stumbling, nearly blind, she climbed out into the open.

The first thing she heard was Mark calling her name.

Her breath chirped voicelessly. She turned, her eyes searching. And then she saw him.

He was standing at the edge of the compound, where the torn security fence dropped away into the forest.

Laughing, almost crying, she called out after him.

Her voice, however, was drowned out by the sound of helicopters.

She saw Mark duck quickly down out of sight, just before she was blinded by spotlights, and the choppers dropped down around her. She heard the sound of boots, and felt hands upon her. When her eyes cleared, she was surrounded by soldiers, two on her arms, calling for medics.

As they sat her down, her eyes stole to the perimeter fence. She caught her last glimpse of Mark Bakker, as he dropped over the top, into the trees, and passed out of sight.

One shout from her and the soldiers would be on him.

So she stood silent as Mark disappeared from her life.

Sally was the only other survivor at the base that night – the *only* survivor as far as General Rhodes knew.

Since then, perhaps with a bit of belated remorse, Rhodes had taken her more directly under his wing.

The General hadn't said as much, but there was a certain punitive measure in their lengthy internment. And while Mark, who had all *kinds* of issues with authority, certainly did *his* part, Sally believed the General now felt responsible.

He greeted her personally when he arrived on the demolished base.

General Nathan Rhodes was an intimidating figure, with a stone face and eyes that looked like mirrors. It was like being comforted by the Sphinx.

"I can't tell you how sorry I am, Miss Crawford," he told her. "You shouldn't have still been there."

And they both knew *why* she was – Mark pissed him off.

Actually, Mark slugged him in the jaw – knocked him on his ass – the very first time they met.

Not Mark's best move, granted. But it *was* after they'd been sequestered for months, first in Mexico, then the States – *then* the world had been destroyed, and it was only after *that* when the gods finally deigned to speak to them.

Not that there wouldn't have been natural friction to begin with. Lifetime military like Rhodes were impatient with civilians. In a world where orders were given and followed, casual insubordination was hard to take, especially in a crisis.

Rhodes explained he would *allow* them to continue living on the base, but impressed upon them the significance of martial law, and, as survivors, they had responsibilities. '*Duty*' was how he put it.

That was when Mark punched him. Sally saw the look of utter shock on Rhodes' face, and hiccupped a hysterical giggle.

It nearly earned Mark a bullet. The two guards drew on him and that would have been the end of it, if not for Rhodes himself, brushing himself off, wiping the blood from his lip, and calling a halt.

"Everybody needs to get knocked on their ass once in a while," he said, dismissively.

Of course, it followed that Mark and Sally were interned for a year, without the formality of further meetings.

A lot *like* being prisoners – just *not*.

And because resources on the base were too strained to allow non-working, non-participating members, civilian, refugee, *or* prisoner, both he and Sally had to work to earn their keep – 'indentured servitude' would not be a gross misrepresentation.

Mark was assigned a lot of maintenance and general labor. Sally, however, worked in the administration office, a position that put her in regular contact with General Rhodes.

Two days after their base was destroyed – once she'd been taken to their latest, makeshift, on-the-fly, traveling 'headquarters' – Rhodes had called her into his office/tent.

"Most of the world's dead," he said. "And I need someone who can type."

He had offered – using the word *'offer'* – a position as his personal assistant.

As it turned out, Sally, wielding general office-skills from working at her college library, was a rare commodity in the new world. In the military, survivors were mostly people who shot guns.

She also wondered if it might be a way of watching after her personally. Rhodes only mentioned Mark indirectly, saying simply that he was sorry for her loss.

Sally was content to let the General believe Mark was dead and gone. For her, the loss was real enough.

And so, for the last six weeks, Sally Crawford, undergraduate co-ed from UCLA, sat at the side of a General, armed with a clipboard and a pen, saying, "*Yes, sir,*" while riding shotgun in jeeps and helicopters.

Today, they were relocating to a new base, referred to generally as *'The Mount'.* Lately, they'd spent a lot of time in transit, as Rhodes supervised each shipment directly, inventorying their remaining arsenal.

The sobering fact was, there wasn't that much left.

Sally had spent most of the Apocalypse sequestered, but ultimately, she still expected there to be *some* kind of official apparatus in place, at least *trying* to deal with it all. She had grown up in a world where there was always someone to *call* in emergencies.

But now Sally was getting a look at how truly dire things had become.

Her demolished compound was salvaged and then abandoned. Over the following days and weeks, they visited a series of storage-sites, arranging transport, as the military regrouped.

As before, these sites brought straggling survivors looking for sanctuary.

But now things had changed.

Official policy, to which Sally was now privy, was based on end-of-the-world extinction-countermeasures.

"Directly from the *eggheads,"* as Rhodes put it.

It was actually the *head* egghead, Dr. Anthony Shriver, who even Rhodes called *Dr. Shrinker.*

New policy regarding refugees was that women of 'productive age' be allowed in.

Their '*most valuable resource*', Rhodes read aloud from the memo.

Men, without some useful skill, would be turned away.

Sally knew Rhodes was following predetermined plans – speculative, and outlined in the safety of the old-world, by teams of academics specializing in 'worst-case-scenarios' – people who the military brass listened to.

Primary among them, the recurring name of Dr. Anthony Shriver appeared on every memo.

For what it was worth, Sally believed Rhodes was only doing his duty as he saw it.

Stabilization was the immediate priority. The Mount was intended to be a permanent home.

More formally, they were calling it the *Arc Project*.

The primary facility was further up in the mountains. Just ahead was a small weigh-station, set up quickly to facilitate transit through the mountains.

Supposedly, the Mount was a long-established survival-bunker, drilled deep into the mountain. According to Rhodes, it was intended to ride out nuclear blasts.

Once the Mount was settled and stability was achieved, that left the next thing on Dr. Shrinker's memo.

Any good survivalist needed a repopulation strategy.

Sally recognized herself as Shriver's 'most valuable resource'.

And she was increasingly under the impression any decisions on the subject were not about to be left up to her.

Sally jumped as the speaker buzzed.

"Heads up, folks," Cap said from the pilot's chair. "We have arrived."

Weaver and Emmett grunted, rubbing their eyes awake.

Cap veered them towards a nearby summit, with a flat plateau, where Sally could see fences and barracks already set-up.

She glanced back, two peaks over, where she'd seen that couple hiding in the forest.

It meant there *was* something else out there.

What if there were more of them?

She remembered how helpless she felt, unable even to shout, at that last moment when she saw

Mark slip over the fence, even as the spotlights zeroed in.

But now it was Mark, yet again, helping her find what she needed in herself. *He* escaped, so she knew it was possible – she had seen it done.

And she had seen other people. Freedom was out there – it existed.

That was enough.

When the helicopter landed, Sally hit the ground running.

# CHAPTER 9

Sally didn't know it, but her first night on the run was much like Mark's had been. She ran blindly through the trees until simply collapsing from exhaustion. She spent the night nestled in the hollow of a tree, with foliage and leaves pulled over on top of her.

All night, she could hear choppers buzzing overhead. Twice, the flash of spotlights passed by.

She didn't remember dozing off, only snapping awake to the brightness of the first sun break, and the chill of the morning.

Physical soreness had set in and she groaned. Nights she'd slept outdoors in her life could be counted on one hand.

Sitting up, she looked over her paltry little pack. She had taken to carrying a little cache of matches, a pocketknife, and the like. But she would need to keep moving, putting distance behind her before she could even risk basic necessities like a fire.

Beyond that, her plan was pretty open. Find some lodgings, scavenge supplies. She knew there was still a lot out there. Unfortunately, she also knew anyone left alive was looking for it too, and those that were left veered strongly into lawlessness.

Then, there was the new wildlife.

That was why Sally waited for the mountains to make her break. She'd heard enough crossfire to know the bigger beasts stuck to the lowlands.

Of course, there was still your typical cougar and bear – all mountain-dwellers.

She would have to find herself a gun. For now, she hiked her pack, and set off downhill.

Her descending path soon brought her to a river. Running alongside the water was a road. It was encroached by overgrowth, but a footpath was cleared away, and it appeared maintained. Her heart pattered with simultaneous excitement and apprehension.

She had seen two people already. There might be an established encampment nearby.

Sally began following the road. The splash of the river joined the tweets of birds as the morning began to fully bloom.

It was the first morning walk, in freedom, Sally had taken in going-on two-years. She was hungry, she was tired, she was afraid, but she'd take it.

Then she rounded the corner, pushing the overgrowth aside, and nearly walked right into a soldier.

The young man turned to stare right at her.

Sally recognized Private Emmett from the chopper. His eyes went wide, and he started to reach for her.

"*Shit!*" Sally blurted, and before she even knew she was going to do it, she extended her hand, palm-first, and thrust it upwards into his nose.

A little trick Mark taught her.

She felt Emmett's nose break. There was a spurt of blood, and he yelped, toppling over backwards, clutching his face.

Sally turned and started to run.

"*Hey!*" Emmett blurted behind her, staggering to his feet, holding his bloody nose. "*Wait!*"

There was the bark of static and she heard him shout into his radio.

"It's her! I've got her!"

Now, Sally heard the clip-clop of his boots as he came after her. Glancing back, she wondered if she should try and ditch into the forest again.

But around the bend, she found another surprise waiting.

Soldiers weren't the only ones on her trail this morning.

Standing in the road, nose to the ground, blocking her path, was an adult *Tyrannosaurus rex*.

The beast reared up and stared at her.

Sally sucked a breath, but instead of a scream, she used it to amp her body into overdrive, turning-heel back the way she came, her voice gasping out like a dog-whistle.

She nearly piled right into Emmett as he chugged after her.

Emmett's eyes were wide, as she screamed into his bloody face, *"Run!"*

She tore away, just as Rexy rounded the corner.

"Holy *shit*," Emmett gawked, letting Sally go, shouldering his rifle.

Sally kept running, knowing not to look back. She'd seen this scenario play out before. For Emmett, it was already too late.

She heard gunshots, followed by an indignant snarl.

Then there was a scream, cut-off by a wet, guillotine chop.

A '*jaw-snap*' was what they called it when crocodiles did it. The sound actually echoed.

Sally looked back to see Rexy toss her head, gulping her meal like a pelican with a fish.

Emmett's severed legs fell off to either side. Swallowing noisily, Rexy bent and snapped those up as well.

Sally turned and ran.

Behind her, more gunfire erupted as Private Emmett's companions arrived on the scene. There was an outraged bellow, and more screams joined the gunfire.

Sally ran with visions of the Devil at her heels, as all the nightmares of days past came flooding back.

Perversely, there was also a sense of betrayal – there weren't supposed to *be* any *T. rex* in the goddamn mountains!

Her body was in instinctual flight – all her earlier soreness and stiffness vanished and she streaked like a jackrabbit.

She screamed aloud when she was snatched bodily off the path and pulled to the ground.

There were suddenly a dozen hands upon her, and she was taken down into the grass. But any breath for another scream was hushed by the touch of spear-tips at her throat.

Sally lay stark-still. Above her, the woman holding the spear nodded to the others.

"It's okay. Let her go."

She looked back down at Sally.

"You'll be quiet, right?"

Sally nodded, wide-eyed, and the hands on her released, pulling her to her feet. She looked around, blinking.

They were all women – Amazons, by the look of them – in torn t-shirts and cut-offs, armed with spears.

And one, Sally noted, who packed a pistol on her hip.

The woman who had spoken smiled grimly.

“I'm Michelle,” she said. “Welcome to Sherwood Forest.”

She nodded back the direction Sally had come, perking her ear to the gunshots and thundering bellows.

“Those bastards have been in the area for weeks,” Michelle said.

Then, as the gunfire faded abruptly into screams, her baleful smile broke into a quick bark of humorless laughter.

“Let’s see how they like our hospitality.”

She held up a rank-smelling towel and tossed it on the trail behind them.

“Rex piss,” she said.

The one with the pistol nudged Michelle's arm urgently, indicating the not-too-distant screams. Michelle nodded, turning to Sally.

“So, are you coming with us or what?”

Sally still hadn’t spoken a word. She glanced back to where the last of the screams now choked away.

She turned back to Michelle and shrugged.

“Okay,” she said.

# CHAPTER 10

Lily sat quietly in a chair outside the makeshift office.

She felt like a schoolchild again, when she had been a regular visitor to the principal.

Or once, when she was thirteen, she'd been caught shoplifting and ushered by the store-manager to the back, sat down in a chair, just like this one, with stern instructions to *'stay put'*, while he called the police.

Lily remembered being frightened that day. Not over being caught, or what her mother or even the police might say – it was more about being dragged back to that dank, dark stockroom.

The store was just a little, local merchant, and the back room was more like someone's unfinished garage – lots of cobwebs, spiders scurrying among the back-stock, with naked bulbs hanging off of open fixtures.

At school, the principal's office was well-lit – it was *'official authority'*, just like the odd trip to the police station.

This was like being kidnapped and taken to someone's basement.

Waiting alone in that back room, twisting her feet, sitting in that simple wooden chair, Lily had thought about running.

She thought about running now.

Back then, fear kept her in place on its own.

Now there was a man outside with a gun.

Last night, she'd fought for all she was worth as she was loaded onto the chopper, enough to wear the patience of the soldier charged with restraining her.

With a muttered, "Hell with this," the young private, *'Weaver'* according to his badge, pressed what looked like a cattle-prod against her leg – the sort of thing bouncers sometimes carried in the rougher clubs back home. Lily was knocked semi-conscious.

In a hazy way, she remembered the pilot, who they called 'Cap', smacking Weaver stiffly across the scalp.

"Is the girl being too rough with you, pal?"

The second soldier, *'Emmett'* on his badge, chided his companion.

"Just get her onboard, Private. Think you can handle that?"

Lily felt herself rolled over and cuffed, then picked-up and carried aboard like luggage. She lay compliantly still until the chopper landed a short time later on one of the nearby peaks.

They were met by an armed escort. There was also a nurse, who promptly stepped forward, ordering Lily's cuffs removed, even as she bent to the mottled scuffs and scrapes along her arms and legs.

The nurse cast a sideways eye at Cap as she dressed Lily's injuries.

"Looks like someone was a little hard on you, honey," she said.

Cap nodded his head towards the other two soldiers exiting the chopper, Weaver with the taser still on his hip.

The nurse, a severe, career-military woman in her forties, waved them off.

"I can handle this," she said. "I'll see her to the infirmary."

Emmett looked doubtful.

"Rhodes said to keep her sequestered until he had a chance to talk with her personally."

The nurse sighed, but nodded.

"Sorry, honey," she said, dabbing alcohol on Lily's face. "You're going to have to go with them. But we can clean you up a bit first."

The nurse took a moment to meet Lily's eyes.

"Just a little heads-up, honey," she said. "Rhodes is old-school. He's a general on the field with his men and he wouldn't have it any other way." She looked at Lily meaningfully. "Things aren't how they used to be, if you take my meaning."

She spent a few minutes doctoring her up, before standing and nodding to Weaver and Emmett. The nurse frowned as they led her off.

Lilly put up no fuss as the two soldiers brought her to a small sequestered barracks, and set her in a room with a simple cot. That was where she spent the night.

In the morning, she was woken by the rush of choppers. Whoever they were searching for was apparently still out there.

Presently, her nurse – '*Price*' from her badge – came to check on her. She ran a cursory eye up and down Lily's bandages, and then nodded.

"You're going to have to come with me, now, honey. The General's been asking about you."

Taking her hand, Nurse Price led Lily through the meandering path of tents, pallets, and equipment to the makeshift-office headquartered at the center of the compound.

She sat Lily in a chair outside.

Private Weaver stood guard. The nurse eyed him sternly, before patting Lily lightly on her shoulder.

"You'll be okay, honey," she said.

Then she left her behind, disappearing in the stir of bodies busily bustling back and forth outside.

Lily looked into the office. The man sitting behind the desk paid no attention to her as he sat scribbling notes and shuffling paperwork.

She was beginning to wonder if he'd forgotten about her, when he set his glasses aside, pushed back from his desk, and waved at her through the mesh window.

"Please," he said. "Come in."

Feeling very much thirteen again, Lily sat down in the chair before his desk. Stepping outside, Weaver shut the door behind them.

Lily swallowed dryly.

"My name is General Nathan Rhodes," the man said. "I'm in charge here." His eyes glanced down to his papers. "You are a civilian, presumed refugee."

Rhodes leaned back in his chair, his face relaxed and benign.

"You aren't out here by yourself," he said. "Who else is in this area?"

Under his scrutinizing eye, Lily actually felt the impulse to just blurt it all out – the shop-lifting kid who just wanted out of trouble. A full confession to the reasonable, friendly good-cop.

She set her lips and forcibly averted her eyes, staring down at her lap.

Rhodes sighed.

"You're being brave," he said. "I respect that."

He tapped sharply on his desk, bringing Lily's eyes back up to meet his own.

"Listen, girl," he said. "No one's going to hurt you, here. But we're in this for the species."

Rhodes' voice was low, rational and confidential.

"You understand, I cannot afford to waste time with you. I have to know what you know."

Lily blinked nervously, but stayed silent.

Rhodes tapped a buzzer on his desk.

"Weaver," he said into it, "send in Nurse Price."

A few minutes later, Private Weaver appeared with the nurse.

This time, she was holding a hypodermic needle.

"Rose?" Rhodes said, and the nurse nodded to Weaver, who abruptly grabbed Lily's shoulders and pinned her arms down.

"Sorry, honey," Nurse Price said.

Lily's eyes blinked wide as the needle stung her neck. In the space of a heartbeat, her head went light and dizzy.

Rhodes appeared sympathetic.

"I understand your position," he said. "You're a brave, loyal girl, and you won't betray your people."

Lily settled into her seat. Now Private Weaver's hands were the only thing holding her upright.

"So," Rhodes continued, "to ease your burden, we will simply remove the element of choice."

Now he smiled confidentially.

"So," he said, "you're *not* alone out here, are you?"

Lily smiled back dreamily, shaking her head, stifling a giggle like a little girl telling secrets.

Somewhere inside her, Lily could feel her core-being crying out – the part that remained aware and awake through the drugged haze, helpless to watch her own actions, like a video-feed from a thousand-miles away.

She heard herself tell all about her sisters, their names, where they came from, favorite color – funny stories.

General Rhodes smiled, cajoling her gently along whenever she started to ramble.

Who knows what else she might have told him, maybe even what happened to Joshua and all their 'men-folk'.

But Rhodes didn't care about any of that. He wanted the here and now.

"Have you seen anyone else in the area?" he asked.

Lily grinned shyly, and now she found herself blushing, discovered in a secret crush.

"There was a man," she said.

Lily smiled.

"A man being chased by a rex."

Rhodes' smile faded into a frown.

And at that very moment, off in the very near-distance, came a bellowing roar.

# CHAPTER 11

Mark really had no plan. He'd already battled the terrain all night and the better part of the day, through miles of hard brush.

But his destination was easy enough to determine. All the choppers were coming and going from a nearby peak, stopping and then moving further on – probably a depot station, not a permanent base.

That was why they hadn't run across Lily's little sisterhood before.

It was, however, still fenced, with guards.

Crouched in the brush, two-hundred-yards from the main gate, Mark weighed his options.

He was wearing a jacket and hat he'd taken from a perimeter guard, creeping up behind the young man, silent as a predator, and clocking him across the back of the head with the butt of his own pistol.

It wasn't like in the movies – he had to hit hard enough to knock him cold, which might be enough to kill him.

*That kind of world*, Mark thought, leaning into his swing. There was the crack of a well-hit hardball, and the guard dropped like a stone.

Mark pocketed his pistol, picking up the unconscious soldier's rifle.

Not that one rifle would be of any particular help versus an entire military base. Did he think he was going to shoot his way in? *And* out?

For a moment, Mark considered simply leaving.

Why go in there? At best, he would get taken back into custody – more likely, dead.

But the answer from his own conscience was inarguable.

He hadn't been able to save Sally. Therefore, he had to go in after Lily, who he'd known all of two days – simple enough.

Did this mean he could forgive himself over Sally?

Of course not.

So, with that inexorable logic in place, all that remained was to go get his ass shot off.

He scanned the perimeter fence, looking for a place to climb. The only other option was to try and bluff his way past the front guard with his uniform.

Mark glanced back after the fallen guard – he heard a rustling.

He blinked. The guard was gone.

There was a heavy *chomp*, and Mark looked up to see Rexy tossing down the guard's whole body like a trout.

The big rex swallowed her mouthful, turning to stare meaningfully at Mark. She almost seemed to smile.

"Oh, *shit.*"

For a half-instant, Mark thought to use the rifle.

Instead, he simply turned and ran.

"*Hey!*" Mark hollered, as he broke out onto the open road, waving his arms.

He saw the armed sentries jolt to attention, just as Rexy burst out of the brush behind him.

There was an immediate response of gunfire.

With a roar that echoed across the surrounding peaks, Rexy charged.

# CHAPTER 12

On the opposite end of the compound, General Rhodes jumped to his feet. When the gunshots were immediately followed by screams, he turned grimly to Private Weaver, indicating Lily.

"Get her quartered-up."

Then he was out the door, already in the fight, barking orders into his radio, as more gunfire erupted just on the other side of the clustered maze of crates and equipment.

Lily stared after him, blinking, still quite high on Nurse Price's chemical cocktail. Then she felt Weaver's hand on her arm.

"Come on, Miss," he said. "I've got to get you someplace safe."

Lily acquiesced affably enough, feeling light as a feather, although she still needed the young soldier's arm for balance, as he took her outside.

Thc sound of gunshots and roars was close. Weaver looked nervously over his shoulder.

Lily remembered his frustrated, angry face when he had tasered her, like a kid worried about getting in trouble, who wasn't messing around anymore. But now, as he gave her a quick shake for attention, his concern seemed genuine enough.

"You stick close, you hear?" he said..

Weaver unshouldered his rifle, holding Lily upright with one hand as he led her towards the back of the compound. The upward slope offered a view of the battle. So far, it was not going well.

Rexy had demolished the perimeter fence and made short work of the guards. Once through, the rows of pallets and trailers were enough to hamper the troops, but the big rex walked right through them.

Lily wasn't sure how bulletproof Rexy really was – she'd seen a lot of shots fired at a lot of *T. rex*, and had yet to see one go down. Part of it was that huge skull and small brain – vulnerable spots were buried deep.

Your aim also had a tendency to suffer under the pressure of five-tons of chomping teeth charging right at you.

That was probably the greatest factor here today – most of the shots were just being scattered at her.

"Come on," Weaver said, pulling Lily along. "You'll be safest in back with the others."

Lily perked briefly through her haze.

"What others?"

"The other civilians," Weaver said, glancing back at the scene behind them. "We're bringing most of the refugees from other areas up to the Mount. The Arc Project."

Lily nodded mildly, and was about to ask more, but was interrupted by a loud electric *zap*.

Weaver's hand suddenly clenched on her arm, and Lily felt a brief connecting shock from his fingers before he fell away.

Without his support, Lilly staggered, but another hand grabbed her arm.

She blinked, confused, but despite the army jacket and hat, it was Mark who caught her, steadying her with one hand, as he held Weaver's own taser over the Private's twitching legs. Mark turned to Lily.

"Jeez," he said, looking into her heavily-dilated eyes. "What did they *give* you?"

Lily pursed her lips thoughtfully.

"I don't know," she said, shaking her head. And then, in a confidential stage-whisper, "but I'm *really* messed-up."

Mark nodded.

"I can see."

With gunshots and a *T. rex* bellowing just over their shoulders, Mark tapped a finger on Lily's chin, holding her attention from her dream-state.

"Lily, listen to me. We gotta get out of here. You need to straighten up or we're not going to make it."

Lily nodded seriously, her face screwing up in a Herculean effort to force back the chemical haze.

Then she relaxed and shrugged.

"Sorry," she said.

Mark sighed.

"Alright, hang on."

Lily felt herself whipped off her feet as Mark grabbed her up and simply started to run. She clutched his shoulders, as her head spun with momentary vertigo.

"Don't drop me!" she chirped, shutting her eyes, tucking her head under his shoulder like a duck under its wing.

With her eyes shut, it was better – the gunshots and bellows were like fireworks, and being carried felt like the shake and pull of a carnival ride.

For a moment, she actually began to dream.

She started back awake as Mark sat her down, and found herself leaning against the wheel of some sort of mini-all-terrain mountain-scooter – the kind Lily used to see on the beaches back home. Mark was trying to get one started.

Lily heard the footsteps before Mark did. Sitting next to him on the ground, she tugged at his jacket.

He turned to the sound of a pistol being cocked.

"Where you taking the lady, soldier?"

Lily recognized the pilot who had flown them in – *'Cap'*.

Mark had a rifle strung over his shoulder, but Cap's pistol was out and aimed. Mark raised his hands.

"You're not army," Cap said.

He looked down at Lily, knelt at Mark's hip, a possessive hand wrapped around his leg.

"You know this guy, do you?"

"He's my friend," Lily said, with a beaming grin.

Cap lowered the gun.

"Got it," he said. He reached into his pocket. "Here, you'll need these."

He tossed a key ring. Mark caught it, blinking disbelievingly.

"Go on," Cap said, "Get out of here."

Gunshots and roaring bellows sounded closer. Cap turned back to the fight.

Mark pulled Lily into the seat beside him and cranked the motor.

"Hang on," he said.

Spinning wheels, he circled the scooter towards the back of the compound, where the fencing was just staked posts and wire – *and* the rear guard had been abandoned to deal with Rexy.

The downhill slope was heavy with brush and very steep – almost a cliff, really.

"Hang on," he said again.

Lily cinched her grip as Mark launched them over the edge into the trees.

# CHAPTER 13

Sally was actually enjoying herself.

How long had it been since she'd had a night out with the girls? A bonfire? Just like the old sorority camp-outs on the beach.

The younger girls did most of the work, like pledges during rush-week. Sally was reminded of her own freshman year.

Back when she was roughing-it, she thought, smiling.

The one named Ginger, who seemed to be the 'older sister', noticed Sally's self-conscious grin and sat down next to her beside the fire. Michelle and Christine joined them.

Christine handed Sally another pint of the smoking potion they'd endowed for most of the evening.

In what seemed a deliberately evocative manner, this apparently ceremonial concoction was stirred in a large, bubbling cauldron, complete with bobbing apples.

It was fruit-flavored, with a strong, but indefinite, aftertaste. It also seemed to carry a mild, mellowing buzz.

Sallow-eyed, soft-featured Luna, she of the aggressive spear-tip, assured Sally it was non-alcohol.

"A herbal tea, actually," she said, smiling softly, as she filled Sally's cup.

That soft smile highlighted a long scar running down Luna's cheek. Sally hadn't noticed during the day, but it stood out in the moving shadows of firelight. It would have been a nasty injury when it happened.

It did seem, she thought, looking around at their little quartet, that they carried the look of alley-fighters.

Sally knew one of their girls was missing, and they had a good idea she'd been taken into military custody.

So far, they were giving Sally time to breathe – she had been immediately pampered, given clean clothes and a for-*God's*-sake, BATH, with a hair-dryer, and a friggin' robe. It was like her first weekend home after living in the dorm her freshman year.

But now, as they all sat down beside the fire, Ginger lay a hand on Sally's wrist, looking her directly in the eye.

"Okay, honey," she said. "Spill it. What's your story?"

Sally was happy enough to oblige – starting with the sinking of the *Pacific Princess*, and ending with the moment she bolted from the chopper into the trees.

"I saw two people on the ground," she said. "A man and a woman."

Ginger nodded.

"Our lost little fawn, I suspect."

"What about the man?" Sally asked. "He wasn't with you?"

"No," Michelle answered equivocally. "We have no men here."

Ginger shook her head... regretfully?

"Not anymore."

Sally wasn't sure she wanted to know, but she asked anyway.

"What happened?"

"Well," Michelle said, shrugging with deliberate apathy, "they just seemed to attract *T. rex*. That tends to get you eaten. It's also the sort of thing that comes down hard on anyone stuck living around you."

Ginger nodded.

"Just like your traveler," she said. "A man that our lost little fawn encountered on the road, and brought back like a lost puppy. "

She eyed Sally meaningfully.

"Another *man*," Ginger said, "who just happened to be being chased by a *T. rex*."

"And now," Michelle added, "with a big rex stalking the territory, along with your General Rhodes, our freedom to search for our lost little sister has been severely handicapped."

There was a tick of silence, broken by Christine, she of the dark, angry eyes and the pistol on her hip.

"We were *safe* here," she said.

Sally heard bitter anger in her voice, reflected in the eyes of all the others.

Luna brought up the other elephant in the room.

"What do you think your military friends will do when they find us?"

*When*. Not *if*.

"Well," Sally replied, "they don't really take refugees anymore. Unless they're women of productive age."

"So," Ginger said, with a wry smile, "we're *in*."

The group of them broke into a cackle of laughter.

"Defenseless women," Ginger said, grinning. "Like us."

The titter faded and now they all eyed Sally seriously.

"After KT-day," Michelle said, "our men presumed to take care of us. And in the manner of men, they stirred conflict, and brought destruction back on us all."

Michelle's brows furrowed with the sternness of a judge.

"It *was* actually almost… Biblical," she said, "Wrath personified."

"A microcosm," Luna offered, "for the whole world. Only we *knew* what brought the dragons down on *our* little tribe."

The scar on her face stood out stark.

"It makes you wonder, what must that transgression have been that brought them down on the whole world?"

Sally looked around at their little circle cautiously.

"*I* never transgressed on anyone," she said, "I'm not being punished for anything. All this just happened to me."

"Really, honey?" Ginger exchanged knowing looks with the others. "I'll bet you can think of *something*."

Sally stared back, uncertainly, suddenly nervous, reminding herself that this was *not*, in fact, an old sorority cook-out.

It occurred to her to wonder who it was she might have crossed paths with – sequestered here on this remote, post-apocalypse mountain pass.

She'd been sequestered on the last facade of the old 'civilized' world – she had no idea how crazy people might have gotten outside.

Ginger put a reassuring hand on Sally's arm.

"Yeah, I know we're crazy," she said, reading Sally's mind. "We're *all* crazy in our own way. You too."

"You don't think this is all God's judgment?"

Ginger smiled.

"They say all things serve the Lord's will, right? Even the Devil." Ginger shrugged. "Isn't the Apocalypse *his* territory? The BIG Dragon. I mean, the world out there's Hell enough for any Devil, isn't it?"

"You could also look at it," Luna said, "as simple opposing forces. Creation versus Destruction. Each has their place. Each has their time."

"And right now," Ginger said, "seems to be the Dragon's time. Might as well learn to ride it."

They all tittered laughter. The hand on Sally's wrist squeezed briefly.

"That's all I'm saying, honey," Ginger said. "Doesn't matter what you call it. We've already had it done to us. The Dragon set down on us all. I'd call *that* Judgment.

"But," she said, holding up a cautionary finger, "that's not the same thing as *Justice*."

"What's Justice?" Sally asked.

"Justice," Michelle said, "is when the Dragon points the right way."

"And *that*," Luna finished, "is the *real* 'Will of God'."

"God*dess*," Ginger corrected, smiling.

Sally absorbed this silently.

In the post-apocalypse, this was certainly not the first time she'd heard the Judgment-day riff. A lot of people called it that, especially at the beginning, when there still *were* a lot of people – KT-day was not an invasion of genetically-bred monstrosities, but actual abominations from the pit.

Not that one didn't feel a lot like the other.

So what was the difference?

A practical devil existed in both scenarios. But one didn't allow for God the Savior – just practical, existential destruction – the absence of hope.

*Devil* with a little 'd'.

An uncomfortable silence settled around the fire. Sally glanced over her shoulder – Serena and the other pledges sat at rapt attention.

"We all suffered," Luna said, her serene face split by its long-running scar. "But the purpose of suffering is that it is a catalyst for change."

Ginger nodded.

"Because of our suffering," she said, squeezing Sally's hand, "we are more than we were before."

Christine and Luna both nodded. There was an approving murmur from Serena and the pledges.

Michelle stood, hefting her spear by her side, her Amazon-eyes severe and purposeful.

"And *that*," she said, "is why we will not submit to your General Rhodes."

For the first time, the taciturn Christine smiled, vicious and dark.

"After the wrath of dragons," she said, pulling her pistol from its holster, "we could hardly fear the wrath of men."

Sally swallowed dryly, nodding clear, deliberate agreement.

Luna rose.

"Come. We have something to show you."

Ginger nodded. Both she and Michelle took Sally's hands.

Sally hesitated, but allowed herself to be pulled from her chair.

She wobbled a little as she stood – that euphoric-tea was giving her a head-rush. Michelle crooked an arm around her, as if expecting it. They followed Luna around the back of the dining-hall, to what looked like a doghouse.

A doghouse for a *big* dog – like maybe a bear-cub.

When she saw what was inside, Sally felt her knees go weak.

If not for the pacifying influence of Luna's smoking-potion, she might have bolted. But Michelle held her still.

Sally had a lot of nightmares about what happened on the beach after the *Pacific Princess* sank, but the worst dreams were of the rex-nest – the hatchlings, no bigger than dogs, swarming on you, chomping out melon-sized bites at a time – too small to hide from.

Luna smiled, kneeling as she coaxed the house's occupant out with a scrap of meat.

"It's okay," Luna said. "Junior's not going to hurt you."

Sally tensed against Michelle's grip, but now Ginger took her other hand.

"This is what we do, girl," she said. "We make *friends*."

At her feet, the little rex-hatchling snapped-up the scraps, then cocked its head, staring up at Sally, as if puzzled by her bizarre reaction.

"No," Sally said, starting to pull away, but Michelle held her fast.

Ginger took Sally's other hand, pulling it down to extend to the rex-pup, like offering for a dog to sniff.

"*Shhhh*," Ginger said. "It's okay. Let him get your scent. Let him know you're one of us."

Sally was paralyzed as Ginger forced her hand down to Junior's scaly snout – the contact was a moment of electric terror.

Now the potion was working against her, conjuring images of bloody, biting teeth.

Junior, for his part, sniffed at her offered hand in a very dog-like manner, although still twitching in that strangely bird-like way. He eyed her suspiciously.

"*Please...*," Sally whispered.

Her head started spinning. That last batch of potion was more potent than before.

Ginger was smiling.

Sally's eyes fluttered, as the spins were replaced by a sense of floating. When she looked down, her hand was still touching the little rex' snout.

Inside, she still wanted to pull away, but allowed Ginger to work her hand over the hatchling's scaly neck – bristly with proto-feathers, a parody of petting a fluffy dog.

The little rex reminded her of a big, scaly parrot. As a kid, Sally knew an old neighbor lady who kept parrots – she remembered how strong and sharp their claws were… and that they would sometimes bite.

Still, the hatchling *seemed* tame, accepting Sally's touch as one accustomed to grooming.

Ginger pulled her hand away, letting Sally pet the little rex on her own.

"Here," she said, handing Sally more scraps. "Give him these."

Sally scratched the hatchling behind its scaly ear, as she fed it the handful of food.

"There you go." Ginger smiled. "See? It's easy to make friends when you have something they want. Ask any dog owner."

Sally wasn't fooled for a moment. She knew the difference. *That* had been a sorority lesson too.

It wasn't '*making friends*'. It was called '*training*'.

Or '*taming*'.

Sally watched herself pet the rex-pup, repressing a shudder of revulsion. Yet, she was helpless to stop, utterly without will.

She fed the last scrap to the baby dragon – little 'd' – and let it lick her fingers, noting how consciously gentle it was with its armament of vicious teeth.

"Your coming here is really quite fortuitous," Ginger said. "You could even look at it as a sign."

She grinned at Michelle, who for once, smiled back.

Sally, despite her inner revulsion, despite every instinct telling her to snatch her hand away from the fanged jaws of this baby dragon, found herself smiling along with the rest of them.

Whatever extra herb was in that last batch of tea, it seemed to leave her particularly susceptible to suggestion.

Was this her first day of 'freedom'?

Sally was again reminded of her first few sorority parties, ragers with neighboring fraternities, with the express purpose of getting the freshman girls drunk and loose, with the full encouragement and beguile of their older sorority sisters.

What was she being loosened-up for tonight?

Ginger tipped back her head, looking into Sally's glazed eyes. She glanced over at the others, nodding.

"I think you're going to be a good sister, Sally," she said.

# CHAPTER 14

The four-wheeler had blown a hole in its gas tank. Mark let it roll until it sputtered to a stop.

He had tried to work his way back to the road, but the terrain took its toll quickly – rocks, large branches. The torn tank drained dry in minutes.

Mark glanced back up the hill. He'd gained them a couple of miles at most.

For the moment, immediate pursuit was unlikely – he could still hear roars and gunshots in the background.

He turned to Lily, sitting beside him, staring up at him dreamily. He sat her back, checking her eyes.

Obviously, Rhodes decided not to waste time grilling her. Mark supposed it was more humane – certainly more pragmatic. After all, what was the point of beating information out of a prisoner, when you could just give 'em a shot, and have a pleasant conversation over tea?

Although, it did mean Lily was not going to be a lot of help for the next several hours, with the dubiously better news that she would likely be awake and ambulatory.

Mark set the dead four-wheeler into park. The scooter was stocked with a first-aid kit and general survival aides, which Mark scooped-up by rote, shoveling them into his pack. He took Lily's hand and pulled her gently onto her feet.

Then he noticed the drip of gasoline, and the trail he'd left behind, probably all the way up to the base.

He could smell gas in the air. The tinder wasn't autumn-dry, but was in spring-bloom. There would be a lot to burn.

Mark debated. He didn't *think* the fire would spread much beyond the immediate peak. Lily's sisters lived high up on the dam, right along the river. They should be fine.

Based on short acquaintance, he also guessed they would generally approve. As he struck a match, he tossed it into his path leading back up to the base.

The flame licked at the gasoline-soaked trail, igniting a crooked path up the hill.

Mark took Lily's arm over his shoulder, taking her weight, and stepping her autopilot-stumble up into a fast walk, as he led them downhill into the trees.

There was the crackle of wet burning leaves behind them, and then the flame reached the four-wheeler's gas-tank. The explosion momentarily drowned-out the battle still raging above.

Mark paused, looking up, listening to the back-and-forth gunfire and responding bellows. It sounded like Rexy was holding her own.

"Come on," he said, pulling Lily along a little faster.

Lily moaned softly. Mark squeezed a reassuring hand on her shoulder.

"It's gonna be okay," he said. "I'm gonna get you home."

But it was not easy-going, especially carrying Lily along. It was nightfall before they reached the bottom of the basin.

Mark estimated another three-miles to go, but for now, he was tired, and he wasn't about to try the forest in the dark.

They stopped at a small stream, an estuary off the main river. Hiking Lily up, carrying her in both arms, he waded across to the far bank. Whenever possible, he liked to camp near water, with his back to a hollow tree or overturned log.

Tonight, it was a piling of branches and flood-brush forced high up on the embankment, creating a comfortable dugout twenty-feet beyond the water. The wind over the moving current would help confuse their scent, and the water itself was too shallow to hide any nasty critters that might be lurking there.

Mark even allowed for a small, leafy fire. The breeze along the water simply added to the aroma of smoke already carried on the air, and the blanket stench over the entire area *should* jam-up Rexy's nose.

He wondered how it worked out with the big mama rex back at the compound.

Mark had gotten a look at her today. This obviously wasn't her first brush with the military. She had fresh bullet wounds riddled across her back, legs and face. But that suggested encounters with individual platoons – small groups with small-arms fire.

Taking on an entire base was something different. Her obsession was quickly becoming self-destructive.

Rexy was lucky small-arms fire was all she'd encountered today. Unlike most common folk, Mark *had* seen a rex or two taken down.

But she had pounced on them where they slept. Man-eating lions made similar raids on caravans, taking advantage of tight-quarters to avoid any meaningful response.

Mark actually smiled a little, wondering what Rhodes' reaction would be, because it was like a strategic move on Rexy's part. Anything big enough to take a Tyrannosaurus down, would be packed in one of those boxed-up crates – not to mention you were talking about the type of weapon you'd be reluctant to fire within the confines of your own barracks.

Still, there had been a lot of gunfire. And while her soft spots might be buried deep, Mark suspected Rexy suffered for her raid today.

*T. rex* was usually not a stupid animal in a general way. They avoided electric fences, and had no history of attacks against heavily-fortified targets. Mark wasn't sure how much Rexy really *knew*, but it seemed like she would *have* to know better than to run, *Hail-Mary*, face-first into gunfire.

All just to get *him*.

Self-destructive obsession. Maybe that was what killed the dinosaurs.

Although, he supposed, you could also see it as a Darwinesque survival mechanism.

It was setting precedent – an evolutionary axiom – a genetic lesson that all other species instinctively knew, or quickly learned.

Don't mess with a *T. rex* – they'll hunt you down.

And *especially* don't mess with a *mama* rex.

Mark saw the wisdom. Given the chance, *he* sure wouldn't do it again.

But it was too late now. He had to come to grips with the fact that she was going to keep coming until one of them was dead.

That made him a lightning rod.

He had to get out of the territory.

But first, they had to get through the night.

Mark spent a little time gathering brush for the fire. Lily lay comfortably among the logjam. The effect of the drugs was finally fading, although her voice was still dreamy.

"Hey," she said, as Mark dropped the last load of kindling next to the fire.

"Hey, yourself," Mark replied, sitting down beside her. He groaned as his body complained at its mistreatment over the course of the day. His shoulders, in particular, were a dull, steady ache.

Lily's eyes were dark in the firelight.

"Thank you for coming after me," she said. "*Really*."

Mark nodded.

"It was the least I could do," he said. "Really."

He felt her hands on his shoulder, rubbing at the knotted muscle.

"You're so stiff," she said. "This is all my fault."

No argument there. Mark shut his eyes. She had good hands, kneading the tired muscle expertly.

A fun-fact from the old-world – Earther chicks gave good back-rubs.

Her hands moved to his neck, rubbing onto his bare skin. Her fingers left an electric crackle in their wake.

Mark was reminded of the *Pacific Princess,* his first night alone with Sally – two years and a lifetime ago. Her touch had been electric, just like this.

Lily's fingers moved further down on his chest.

The knead became a caress.

For a second too long, Mark allowed it to happen, and then he felt her lips touch at his neck – a peck of teeth.

He reached up to clasp her hand, to stop her, and as he turned, she slid herself into his arms.

What was the look he thought he had seen in her eyes?

Innocence?

Except that wasn't it. It was the innocence of an animal in the woods.

What he really meant was… *feral.*

*Wild.*

"We shouldn't do this," he said, as her hands lit lightly around his neck.

Her breath was heavy, her eyes low.

"*Shouldn't* we?" she said.

She pulled him down beside her.

After that, the last of his resistance was gone. Mark shut his eyes and surrendered to the moment.

# CHAPTER 15

In the morning, they broke camp and began to make their way back.

Mark woke to find Lily already up, bustling about, poking at the fire, the soul of domesticity around their fourteen-square-foot campsite. She smiled when she saw him awake. Mark found himself smiling back.

Being with her was not what he expected – the girl was *definitely* not innocent.

She talked for a little while afterward, nestled under his arm. In the afterglow, she seemed to fall into a sort of confessional state, clinging to him as if she were afraid he might bolt.

He kept his hands on her, touching lightly, reassurance that he wasn't going anywhere.

Perhaps not entirely true, but he was content to cross that bridge in the morning. So he listened, nodded, and made encouraging sounds, waiting for her to sleep.

Mark did learn a few things – for example, he apparently reminded Lily a lot of '*Joshua*', leader of Ginger and Michelle's 'wolf-pack'.

The one that had been taken by the rex.

Lily's secret crush, of course.

All at once, she started to cry.

"I *saw*, when the rex took him," she said, as if suddenly reliving it. "I saw… its *teeth*…"

A bad topic for drug-tripping. Mark patted her cheek.

"Hey," he interrupted. "Maybe we could change the subject."

Lily shook her head, as if not hearing him.

"I didn't hate them," she said, tears running. "I knew why they came."

Her fingers dug ever so slightly into Mark's shoulder. Her next words were a whisper and brought the slightest shiver up Mark's spine.

"A mother's rage."

Lily fell silent, the storm of tears drying on her cheek. For a long time, the only sound was the crackle of the fire, just over the bubble of the stream.

Just the sort of thing that could mask ponderous, yet stealthy footsteps.

Primitive man once had these same fears – humanity had come full circle.

Except, Mark thought, what in human history could have actually been worse than this? Than right now?

By the time the earliest human ancestors ventured outside their caves, the dragons were long gone. Sure, they had lions and tigers and bears. There were sharks and crocodiles. And all these modern monsters were certainly scary enough, even inspiring worship – a perverse side-effect of the human condition. Historically, crocodiles were more worshiped than Jesus, no matter how many women and children they snatched from the riverbanks.

And of course, snakes – the tempter of Eve.

So what brand-new religion might be brewing, percolating, at the dragons' feet? What placation?

For what really was worship but buying a karmic bargain with fate? Pleading to the crocodile to leave your women and children alone by the riverbank.

In that light, you could see the serpent's appeal to Eve.

And then out of the silence, as if responding to his thoughts, Lily stirred, her voice slurred as if she had already started to dream, while still clinging to a caffeine-stimulated consciousness.

"She saved us today, you know."

Mark glanced down at her – was she talking about Rexy?

Lily's eyelids dipped as she finally began to slip into slumber.

She blinked, and for a moment, she was dreaming awake. Mark caught one last little whisper.

"Can't fight a rex. Gotta get them to just *do* it."

Lily nodded as if someone in her dream-world had answered.

"I think," she said, "Joshua realized that too late."

Then she settled into a soft little snore.

But her words hung in the air and now Mark found himself sitting awake.

Lily was right – without Rexy, both of them would probably be either captive or dead.

Mark wondered again the extent of the big rex' intelligence. Would she appreciate the irony?

He also agreed with Lily on another point – he *didn't* hate Rexy. He understood her side.

Just like Lily's rex-pack – she knew *why* they had come.

Mark also noted the personal terms Lily used to describe the big rex.

A psychological coping mechanism – make friends with what hurt you.

Even more than that, spiritually bonding with it.

Pretty soon, you were praying to the crocodile. Placating the dragon.

He had seen how Lily was with the hatchling, how it responded to treats, imprinting upon her and her sisters.

They had themselves a puppy – a group of sorority sisters with a pet pit-bull in their apartment for protection. They were training themselves a watchdog.

Or in this case, a guardian dragon.

In the absence of Adam, this tribe of Eves were perfectly content to embrace the serpent.

After all, what good had Adam ever been, anyway?

In fact, *their* tribe of Adams apparently picked a fight with a whole rex-pack. Lily and her sisters clearly recognized the fact that Mark had a rex on his own tail as something that had blown back on them before.

Mark looked down at Lily nestled under his arm. Rescuing her meant finishing the job.

He decided right then that he would take her home in the morning, and then be gone.

With Lily cuddled beside him, Mark slept well, and didn't stir until the first ray of dawn.

Once the sun was up, they broke camp, kicked out the fire, and started off the last few miles to the dam. Rather than trying to find the road, they just simply followed the stream.

They walked without talking. Lily strolled along the water, admiring the cobbled rocks, letting the breeze blow her hair. Her flouncing gait was different this morning. Today was a lazy stroll, crossing Mark's own path every dozen steps, for a possessive pat or touch.

Presently, the dam came into view, as the stream joined the main river.

Lily squeezed against him, pulling his hand.

But now Mark stopped.

Lily turned.

"What?"

Mark shook his head. "This is as far as I go."

Lily's brows furrowed.

"What are you talking about?"

"You got caught following me. That meant it was my fault. So it was up to me to bring you home." Mark indicated the dam. "Here's home."

Lily dropped his hand, staring back disbelievingly.

"I'm sorry," Mark said, "but you know I can't stay."

"Are you kidding me?" Lily said, stepping back, hands doubled into fists. Mark expected resistance, only wondering what form it would take – answered now, as Lily's face darkened in anger.

"What about last night?" she demanded.

Mark shrugged – a gesture intended as a precursor to an explanation, but was clearly taken as an answer itself – and not taken well, because before he could even speak, Lily was on him, swinging, cursing, spitting.

"How *dare* you?"

"I'm sorry!" he shouted, grabbing her arms. "I shouldn't have let it happen. Just listen…"

Mark held her still.

"Please," he said. "This is me trying to be responsible. That big rex is still out there, and it's going to track me. I'm not safe to be around. When I leave the area, she'll follow."

Lily was crying now, no longer fighting, shaking her head.

"She'll kill you."

Slowly, Mark let her go, stepping away. She stared back, her face torn between anger and tears.

"If I can make it out of the mountains," Mark said, "I can find a rig, and once I get on the road, I can leave her behind."

Lily shook her head, tears running, her face angry and stubborn.

"I'm sorry," Mark said. "I've got to go."

"You're not leaving," Lily said defiantly.

Mark held up his hands.

"Please. Don't try to stop me."

He started to back up, waiting to see if she would follow. But she only stood there, staring back, implacably.

"Goodbye, Lily," he said.

Deliberately, he turned and began to walk.

He heard the crunch of brush as she stepped up behind him.

With a sigh, he turned, just as she pressed the taser against his chest.

Mark had time to wonder when she had grabbed it, then there was the smell of ozone and an electric *zap*, as he was knocked bodily to the ground.

Lily's dark eyes were now grim and purposeful.

“Joshua didn’t know how to handle a rex, either.”

Lily stood over Mark, as he writhed on the ground.

“The trick,” she said, “is to make friends. And how do you do that? You give them what they want. Just like giving a dog biscuits.”

Lily smiled.

“All we wanted was to make friends,” she said. “All the rex wanted was Joshua.”

She shrugged.

“And that’s what *really* happened to them.”

Lily leaned over, holding the taser.

“We just ran out of biscuits.”

She pressed the taser against his chest. Mark kicked, jerking on the ground like a fish.

A third zap knocked him out.

# CHAPTER 16

Sally came awake slowly, like a drunk that hasn't quite slept it off. She was foggy on where she was as Ginger gently prodded her awake.

"Come on, honey," Ginger said. "Time to get you ready for the ball."

Sally was about ask what *that* meant, when the world abruptly spun in a psychedelic blur. She lurched, nearly falling out of the small bed, where she had apparently been laid down for the night.

Ginger smiled, moving to steady her.

Sally felt herself propped upright, and was now aware of others in the room. Serena and another girl were attentive handmaidens at her side, primping her face and hair.

As her blurry eyes focused on the second girl, Sally blinked in recognition.

"It was *you*," Sally said, dreamily. "On the ground."

The girl paused, looking uncertain. Ginger lay a calming hand on Sally's shoulder.

"This is Lily," she said, smiling. "She was our lost little fawn. Led astray by a wayward, wandering fox."

Ginger looked down at Lily, semi-reproachfully.

"Weren't you, dear?"

Lily looked appropriately mollified. Ginger patted her shoulder as well.

"It's alright," she said. "It's all worked out well."

Sally blinked slowly.

Lured by a 'fox'? That meant the man Sally had seen with her.

A man running from the military.

*And* from a rex.

Through the dreamy haze, she actually managed an ironic smile. She had seen Mark's face in every stray refugee they'd encountered for the last couple months.

*Of course* it looked like him on the ground. Why wouldn't it?

There was a tap at the door. In her internal slow-motion world, Sally turned as Michelle seemed to float into the room.

"We're ready," Michelle said.

Sally blinked with detached, yet over-observant focus, noting that Michelle's earthy, surfer-girl rags were now a full-body robe, with a hood – basic black.

The two handmaidens were both clad in white versions of the same cut.

*Pledges*, Sally thought distantly.

Outside, it was just getting dark. The last thing she remembered was seeing midnight. She'd lost an entire day.

As the rising full moon cast eldritch light, she could hear the reedy-notes of a flute playing in the background.

Her handmaidens applied the last touch-ups. Lily daubed white make-up on her face, followed by patterns of black. Serena finished with her hair, tying it all back with a black velvet band.

Looking down at herself, Sally realized she, too, was clad in a hooded robe – hers was bright red.

Ginger gently pulled the hood over Sally's head, taking special care not to muss her hair. Serena and Lily pulled her onto her feet. She felt remarkably light, like her toes were the only thing holding her on the ground, and if she let go, she would simply float away.

Michelle leaned back out the door.

"She's ready," she called.

Sally heard the approving murmur of a crowd outside.

With her attentive handmaidens guiding the way, she was now led out from the rear of the compound, through the business offices, into the main saw-yard.

The last twilight had faded, and the grounds were lit by firelight. The dam was adorned in torches.

Gathered in the yard below, the white-robed pledges kneeled, bowing their heads, as Sally was escorted past.

Waiting at the pulpit atop the dam, adorned in black, were the big-sisters. Luna stood with a book in hand. Christine was the minstrel Sally had heard, but now she set her flute aside.

The modern industry of cranes and working elevators took on an unearthly glamour in the torchlight. By day, the platform was a practical, almost reassuring relic of technology, the rational world of the too-recent past. But with the passage of hours and a rotation of the Earth, it doubled nicely as a pagan sacrificial altar.

And that's what this *was*, wasn't it?

Sally began to be afraid.

But her will to resist seemed to be gone. She sat at Luna's feet, Serena and Lily's hands pushing her down lightly, like a balloon.

With a flourish, Luna stepped aside, revealing the open elevator-shaft behind her.

Sitting in the cage, its broken-leg still sporting its cast, and bundled-up like a toddler, was the little hatchling rex.

Luna made a motion with her hand, as if offering a dog a treat. Junior responded with a warbling howl.

Sally shrank back, her fear cutting through the physical apathy, but Michelle and Ginger's hands joined the others, keeping her still.

"Are you going to kill me?" Sally breathed softly, tears threatening the psychedelic daze.

Ginger's reassuring hand rubbed her shoulder.

"Oh, honey," she said, laughing, "of course, not. We want you to be *one* of us.

"But," she added, leaning close, "joining our Coven requires an initiation."

Coven? Sally blinked through the dreamy haze.

"You're... *witches?*" Sally asked.

"That's a slur," Ginger returned quickly. "An archaic term, created by male-dominated propaganda disguised as religion, used to justify persecution and slaughter of thousands."

"As Devil-worshipers," Luna added. "But they mostly targeted simple holistic healers, midwives and the like. Almost none of the women condemned as witches were anything like Devil-worshipers."

Sally's glazed eyes turned to the baby dragon wrapped in his blanket, sitting on a pedestal in its place of honor.

"But...," she said slowly, "*you* are. Right?"

Ginger knelt and patted the baby dragon.

"It's *his* time," she said, smiling.

Junior purred.

"The Devil," Ginger said, turning back to Sally, "always gets his due."

She leaned forward.

"A sacrifice personal to *you*."

The pledges watched avidly. Michelle, Christine and the other elders were fixed upon her.

Sally looked up and now realized the arm of the crane had been turned, reaching out over the edge of the dam. There was another elevator car hanging from the cable, dangling over the hundred-foot drop.

She could see a man inside.

A young man she *knew*.

Sally had seen him on the ground – the 'fox' who had come back to the village with Lily.

Of *course*, it looked like Mark – why wouldn't it?

Sally was beginning to understand.

The trickle of a tear blurred the black and white skull that had been painted onto her face.

"Is this what happened to *your* men?" she asked, blankly.

Ginger smiled.

"Joshua and his wolf-pack were old-school," she said. "They had to be purged."

Ginger looked grim.

"That," she said, "was a sacrifice personal to *us*."

The others nodded soberly.

There followed a tick of silence.

It was broken by Lily, her attentive handmaiden – quiet, soft, but in words louder than Sally had ever heard.

"Some of us," she said, "had their children."

Lily nodded meaningfully to Serena – her pledge-sister's face had gone dark and haunted, turning away quickly when Sally met her eye.

Despite the dream-like fog, Sally caught the insinuation well enough.

There were no men here.

Nor were there any of the *children* of these men.

How many? Sally wondered, looking around the room.

"A sacrifice," Luna said, "personal to *us*."

Sally stared back in helpless, drug-induced apathy.

"What do you want from me?"

Luna nodded to the others. Michelle placed a heavy-duty hunting knife in Sally's hand.

Christine raised her flute and began to play.

As if in trained-response, the hatchling rex stirred, and began to shriek out loud, imitating the notes. Its cries echoed in the riverbed below.

And somewhere, indistinct and directionless, there was a distant, answering *roar*.

An angry mother calling to a lost, and perhaps stolen child.

# CHAPTER 17

Mark was a bit scared of heights – not climbing trees, or rocks, where he had a sure-grip on something solid – more like just the sort of dead-drop he found himself dangling over now.

He had awakened to find himself looking a hundred-feet straight down into the basin. He was locked in what was, apparently, a secondary elevator-car, adapted into a shark-cage, swinging from the arm of the crane, stretched out over the edge of the dam.

Mark could also see inside the elevator itself. Nestled princely in a pile of blankets, was Junior, Rexy's hatchling.

And all along the edge of the dam, adorned in robes, holding torches, were the whole flock of these nutcase mountain… well, *witches*, apparently.

Funny thing – he'd grown-up in the northwest, which had Wiccans and witches to spare – and he had been scolded more than once, by girls he knew in high school, over negative associations attached to what was, in modern-days, mostly considered an earthy-type religion.

But there were *bad* witches too.

Mark was always assured that was discouraged because whatever evil you cast would come back three-times on you.

Supposedly.

Mark, however, took that sort of rule like the warning-label on a pack of cigarettes – people did it anyway.

It also might not count in cases of ritual and sacrifice, which seemed to be scheduled tonight.

He'd watched them set up for the last couple of hours. At first, he shouted over, but long since gave up.

The moment the sun dipped over the horizon, they lit the torches.

Ironically, Mark was reminded of his one Christmas on campus – the fraternity dives versus the sorority palaces – the way the girls would accessorize mundane surroundings. In this case, the functional utility of the sawmill was quite convincingly re-purposed as a pagan ritual-site.

The elevator was the altar, with Junior seated in the position of honor. The younger girls, robed in white and lined in concentric circles, kneeled, hands folded in the semblance of prayer.

Mark saw Lily up front, no doubt a privilege she was afforded, like when she first brought him home to – or *for* – dinner.

It was dark, but Mark could still see her eyes, wide and dilated, reflecting like a cat's. This was the feral pixie he'd met last night.

Standing on the platform, clad in elders' black, Christine started-up again on the flute – this time, sharp, chirping notes the hatchling *T. rex* in the elevator-cage immediately answered with loud squawks.

Luna pushed the button, and the grinding metal gears lurched to life. The cage began to drop. When it was halfway down, Luna stopped the car.

Junior's cries echoed off the dam wall into the basin.

Now Michelle tossed what looked like a bunch of torn towels over the edge. Mark frowned, puzzled, until the rank odor reached him.

*Rex piss*, he realized.

Just like those torn rags he'd seen his first day in the mountain.

There was a murmur from the sorority pledges as the elder sisters prepared the tribute.

Christine narrated with a lively theme on her flute.

Then, with a motion from Luna, Christine stopped.

Pulling a knife from her belt, Christine approached a lone figure, cloaked in red, kneeling before the altar – the shape of a woman, unrecognizable in black-and-white face paint.

Mark *did* recognize Ginger, diminutive, yet lithe in her own black robe, as she raised the red-garbed woman's hand to the altar.

Christine placed the knife in her outstretched palm.

Luna stepped aside so the woman in red and Mark could see each other.

Her make-up was the face of a skull.

And was it just the expression they had painted there, or did the eyes staring out look utterly terrified?

There was no such look in Ginger's eye. Deliberately, she closed the painted woman's hand over the hilt of the knife.

Luna waited at the makeshift altar, where a rope had been secured from the crane to the elevator platform. As Luna pulled lightly on the line, Mark felt his cage rock.

Now, as Mark looked more closely, he realized they had rigged a rope through the cables holding his cage. Cutting the rope would drop him into the ravine.

Why go to all *that* trouble? Why not just use the controls on the crane itself?

But the answer presented itself as he simply looked around – the reason was the same as the pageantry of the ritual itself.

They wanted to end his life with the cut of a blade.

The woman in red waited silently, knife in hand. She seemed to sway, like a cobra entranced by a charmer.

Was she injured? Her face was made-up, but she did not appear elderly. Drugged, perhaps?

After a moment, Michelle took her by the wrist, like a parent teaching a child silverware, and placed her knife's edge on the rope holding Mark's cage.

In the basin below, Junior's piping cries echoed.

And then, from out of the darkness, something answered.

First, there was that guttural *'ahem'* Mark had learned to associate with Rexy, subtly announcing her presence, but not her direction – a little grunt she used, just drifting it out on the wind, to scare-up movement – and it always seemed to come from nowhere.

But the echoing crash that followed solved that.

It was the sound of a collapsing dead-fall – huge, elephantine legs, kicking aside human-sized barriers like toys. Just like the dead-fall that guarded passage to the dam in the basin below.

Except this sound did not echo up from the basin. Nor were these rolling logs.

This was the dead-fall of boulders that had been blown out of the hillside into the road behind the mill – the path that led up into the mountain.

There was dead silence in the saw-yard.

Christine's flute rolled on the ground, and Mark saw her pistol out and drawn. Simultaneously, Luna reached out and pushed the gun back down to her side.

The robed figures turned, falling aside like dominos as a massive shadow separated from the two-story buildings at the rear of the compound like a tiger parting through long strands of grass.

With that slow, stalking pad, that deliberate, silent gait that carried the weight of a dragon, Rexy stepped into the open.

# CHAPTER 18

The Coven stared back, aghast, frozen still.

Junior's honking cries echoed in the basin below.

And right in Rexy's sights, Mark dangled like a lure on a line.

Despite everything, he couldn't help but marvel at the stubbornness of this beast.

He himself had navigated the terrain beyond the sawmill. After Lily was abducted, he'd circled around to avoid the village, and found a near-vertical climb. How had this five-ton walking tank managed?

Mark once saw an elk, a tank of a deer, probably close to a thousand-pounds, run up a thirty-foot embankment that had taken him fifteen-minutes to climb.

Was it possible he was still underestimating her *that* much?

Whatever the case, Rexy had flanked them, the classic predator strategy of approaching from the rear.

But what now would be her target?

The white-robed fledglings fell aside, clearing the path to the altar. The woman in red sat frozen, both rope and knife in hand, while above her, Luna and Christine stood poised. Michelle hovered protectively, just behind.

Rexy's head cocked, regarding this strange tableau, as well as the conflicting scents of both Mark and her own young.

Ginger's voice was deliberately hushed.

"The cage," she said. "We need to bring the cage back over."

But that was when Rexy moved forward.

The bleating of her lost offspring echoed, and the scent was near, but the elevator-car had been lowered out of sight.

That left Mark, hanging over the edge of the dam, just out of reach.

Ginger hissed, pointing to the crane. Michelle nodded, and started edging her way over.

But she was forced to jump aside as Rexy, ignoring her completely, suddenly lunged after the proffered bit of live-bait hanging from the cable.

Mark saw her coming. The massive skull split, tooth-studded jaws gaping – an image he'd seen in nightmares, even before this half-psychotic dragon-beast set itself on his tail.

He shrank back helplessly, pressing against the bars as five-foot jaws with banana-sized teeth yawned forward and snapped shut a bare meter short.

The cage was *just* out of her reach.

Not that she wouldn't keep *trying*.

Rexy barked a belligerent, frustrated roar, stamping her feet, cracking the cement along the edge of the dam with the impact.

Then she lunged forward again, this time snapping her jaws within two-feet.

She stumbled slightly on the precipice.

Ginger turned to Luna, and Mark heard real concern in her voice.

"She's going to fall."

Cautiously, moving right past Rexy's stomping feet, Luna climbed back up on the platform and pushed the elevator button. The screeching cables now began pulling the cage back up towards the top.

Junior, who had fallen silent at the sound of his matron, started bleating once more.

Rexy took another chomp at Mark's cage. This time, one of the banana-like teeth clipped two of the bars.

The offhand snap *cleaved* them.

That was a big difference between *Tyrannosaurus* and the other big meat-eaters. Most theropods had knife-blade-teeth. Tyrannosaur-teeth were armor-piercing spikes. Other big carnivores left long, jagged, razor-wounds. *T. rex* bit out *holes*.

If Rexy caught the cage, she would bite through it like a Great White shark chomping a surfboard.

The glancing impact left the dangling elevator-car spinning, and might have brought it within reach on the back-swing, except that the jury-rigged rope, holding the whole contraption to the altar, slipped. The slack fed out with a heart-stopping five-meter drop.

But the cable itself had not been released, and it caught, jerking the car to a jarring stop.

Rexy leaned forward, precariously balanced, her target suddenly further away than before. Again, she stamped angrily, and now the entire platform began to rattle.

Ginger pulled the woman in red aside. Luna jumped away from the shaking platform. Michelle was perched, waiting for a shot at the crane's operator seat. Christine crouched beside Ginger with her pistol drawn, although wisely had yet to fire a shot.

The elevator car reached the top and the door opened.

Inside, Junior cawed loudly.

Rexy's attention turned from the precipice to the elevator. The saw-yard fell silent as she nosed the hatchling.

In the moment Rexy's attention turned to her offspring, Michelle made a dash past her, skittering lithely up the side of the crane into the driver's seat. She turned the key in the ignition.

There were two sputtering kicks from the old engine and the great mechanical beast roared alive.

Ironic, Mark thought, in the chaotic moments that immediately followed – it was a well-meant gesture. At least, as far as Rexy was concerned.

Hell, they were *worried* about her. They were trying to be *accommodating* – they wanted to feed Mark to her right there on the safety of the goddamn dock.

Unfortunately, *T. rex* tended on the touchy side, and starting-up the crane turned out to be a bad move. The growl of the engine, right in her ear, startled the big rex, who had now been put into the presence of a hatchling.

The result was predictable enough – Rexy turned and attacked.

Before Michelle even begun to swing the cage back over safe ground, the massive jaws latched onto the crane's heavy-duty steel-arm like a vice.

A single shake, like a bulldog with a bone, and the mechanical limb was torn out of joint.

The cage threatened to simply rattle off the cable, or maybe break open like a piñata as it slammed against the side of the dam, before once again swinging out wide over open space.

Inside, Mark was knocked dizzy. Up top, he heard Michelle cursing as the crane started to lean over the edge. Worse, the platform itself began to tilt.

Mark could feel the slow drag as the crane's balance listed like a sailboat in a soft, but sneaky crosswind.

Apparently unsatisfied, Rexy kicked at the crippled rig, tipping it on one side with a heavy *boom* – dropping the cage another several meters straight down.

Mark grunted at the jarring impact. Careening his head upwards, he saw Michelle leap clear of the operator's seat, as the fallen crane tilted at the edge of the shaking platform.

"Get clear!" Michelle shouted, waving Luna and Christine back. Ginger pulled the woman in red off of the altar and they all fell away together.

Rexy turned from the toppled crane, looking over the edge of the dam after Mark, still dangling tantalizingly below. She clearly associated him with the metal creature that just threatened her and her infant.

Junior scowled indignantly.

Mark wondered what passed for thought in the big rex' head. He could see her mind working. Mark was out of reach. So what now?

After a moment, her massive foot came down on the inert crane, sending the cage spinning.

If a *T. rex* could smile, Rexy did now. She kicked again. A couple more would probably be enough to finally knock it all loose, down into the basin.

Mark was sure Rexy would have preferred to sink her teeth into him, but she would settle for him simply being dead.

Rexy coiled for another kick. Mark shut his eyes.

That was when the entire site suddenly lit up in blinding lights.

There was a rushing wind-blast and the roar of rotor-blades as military choppers descended down upon the saw-yard.

Promptly, all hell broke loose.

# CHAPTER 19

In the eleven months since KT-day, Cap had toured extensively as a pilot, in a lot of hot-spots, and he'd seen a rex or two taken out.

The guns they brought this time *ought* to be up to the job. The mission tonight was to put that animal down.

Rexy had done a lot of damage at the depot-base yesterday. There was no headcount yet, but casualties were as high as any single incident Cap had ever heard of, certainly involving just one animal. That was not to mention lost supplies, irreplaceable these days – vehicles, food, weapons – and somehow a fire had gotten started that was currently burning down the south flank of the mountain.

It was General Rhodes himself who fired the tracker-dart into Rexy's back as the big rex left his compound in ruin, stomping off in seeming frustration, retreating into the forest, utterly careless to the destruction she'd left behind.

Rhodes hadn't even waited to see if the dart stuck, before he turned to the first soldier closest, and said, "I want that animal destroyed, by close of business tomorrow."

That nameless soldier had bolted, reporting immediately to his superiors.

Cap had to hand it to Rhodes – he ran a tight ship. Within minutes, the operation was in place, even as they put out their own fires, dealing with the wounded and the dead.

Rhodes had given them one day. As it turned out, it was going to be close.

They tracked the rex' signal and were coming in with four choppers – a pair of gunners, and two birds loaded with heavily-armed troops.

They had already known about the sawmill at the top of the dam. Lily's drug-induced testimonial filled in the gaps about the rest.

The subject of that young woman's escape had not yet come up, although Cap was sure Rhodes hadn't forgotten. Private Weaver, currently riding gunner, reported being hit with his own taser.

Cap wondered what the reaction might be, should his own role in the young lady's escape come to light. Not that he planned to put it on the record.

It might, however, be a short-lived escape. If Lily made it home, it was probably here.

Kind of a hippie-commune was how Rhodes described it – women only.

Who, according to Dr. Shrinker's last memo, were their most vital resource.

And right now, according to their signal, that rex was almost directly on-site.

If that big rex went through the village like it had their base…?

Well, there just wouldn't be anyone left alive. Cap would have helped that girl escape home to die.

Rhodes' instructions were succinct.

"Minimize collateral and protect civilians. But bring that animal down."

Got it. Shoot. But be careful.

But as Cap was about to discover, that would have required at least passing cooperation from the civilians on the ground.

That was not to be the case.

Sally saw them coming as they crested the hill, and wished she could have cried a warning.

She felt the blast of wind from the choppers a moment before the eruption of machine-gun fire – answered in a heartbeat by an outraged, agonized bellow as the shells tore into Rexy’s thick hide.

The chemical dream-state magnified it all to nightmarish proportions, yet Sally stared as passively as if watching it on television.

Helpless in her own body, Sally screamed silently in her head.

Ginger’s hands wrapped around her protectively as she and the rest of the Coven simply fell back.

This wasn’t going to be a battle that lasted long.

The first blast of gunfire had been telling. Rexy was staggered. The shells tore her open across her rib-cage into the upper thigh.

Rexy turned to face the second chopper as it made its pass.

This time she attacked first.

The pilot swerved to avoid the snapping jaws, but threw his gunner off target. This blast scorched the big rex along its back and tail – painful, but flesh wounds.

Not that you’d know it, listening to Rexy's outraged snarls.

But Sally also heard her choke – the wet sound of blood in the lungs.

The other two choppers landed in the saw-yard behind them, spilling out troops to either side, armed with heavy-duty hand-rifles.

One soldier kneeled down with a LAW rocket-launcher on his shoulder.

To Sally's half-passive eye, it actually looked rather cartoonish – when it fired from the troop's shoulder it launched like a giant bottle-rocket.

The blast knocked Rexy bodily off her feet. The shell missed her broadside, glancing off her hip, but bones were shattered and she crashed down onto her side with a heavy, guttural, "*Whuff!*"

Christine, with her pistol already drawn, now stood, her expression going blank and deadly.

She drew a bead and shot the rocket-gunner through the heart.

Sally heard a startled curse from the man's fellows. "What the *hell*?"

Christine opened up on the rest of them, dropping two more, before the others fell back under cover. Sally saw rifles turning in their direction.

As the first chopper circled back, Sally suddenly found her will through the toxic haze.

With a sudden lurch, she pulled free of Ginger's protective grip, and caught Christine by the wrist, wrestling for the gun.

Christine smirked.

"Valley girl," she spat, as she quickly muscled Sally back down.

To be fair, the deciding factor was probably high-levels of narcotics, but Christine made the most of it, bringing the pistol-butt against the back of Sally's head, knocking her semi-conscious.

With a grim smile, Christine turned back towards the incoming chopper and opened fire.

Seeing the shot, Cap cranked the lever, pulling them away, but a bullet still punched through his windshield. Behind him, Private Weaver yelped as shrapnel bounced off his cheek. He wiped away blood.

"What the hell was that?"

Cap yanked the chopper hard to the right.

"That crazy bitch is shooting at us!"

Weaver turned his guns downwards.

Cap cranked the lever, just as the Private pressed the trigger. The stream of shots went wild, launching into the air, leaving tracers like lasers.

"Hold your fire, God damn it!" Cap ordered.

"She's shooting at us!"

"With a pistol! We're in a chopper! I'm going to pull back!"

Cap banked hard. He had been starting another pass at the rex, but it looked like the beast was down anyway. That rocket-blast had left a cratered wound across her lower back.

Who would have guessed that the creature would still be able to lunge, from a prone position, launching its five-tons into the air, and latch its massive jaws onto their undercarriage as the chopper passed?

The chopper was given a terrific, violent shake. Cap heard Private Weaver grunt as he was slammed against the compartment wall, and lay stunned.

Cap wrestled with the controls, but there was no chance at all. Rexy swung the chopper into the platform.

The fuel tanks exploded on impact.
After a moment, the ammo did too.

# CHAPTER 20

Trapped in his cage, Mark saw the conflagration above – the bursting flames, the rattle of artillery shells firing spontaneously. He heard an agonized roar as modern machinery chopped and burned prehistoric flesh. Mark could *smell* it.

The entire platform was finally breaking away. Mark could hear Junior's outraged caterwauling as the elevator-car slipped its moorings, sliding downward on its tracks, the cable flopping loose.

Then there was an even louder metal shriek as a bend in the shaft briefly ground the elevator's gears to a halt, stopping the elevator car halfway down, nearly eye-to-eye with Mark himself.

Junior regarded Mark balefully.

Incredibly, the little rex took a snap at him, bum-leg and all, reaching its little head through the bars.

Then Mark's cage dropped a few more feet as the cable began to slip. He was still fifty-feet above the rocks.

The burning chopper tilted on the remains of the platform.

Rexy, broken and burned by the blast, nevertheless clung doggedly to the chopper's undercarriage, despite the burning flames.

Then there was another massive blast – another LAW missile.

This shell hit her clean, and blasted Rexy over the edge.

She took the entire platform with her, the crane, elevator, and dragging the remains of the chopper still latched in her jaws.

For one seemingly time-lapsed moment, it all seemed to hang together, Rexy poised, clinging to the wreckage, levitating in utter defiance of gravity.

Then, her five-tons began to tumble down.

The last moorings broke away as Rexy pulled the platform with her. The elevator-shaft separated, sending the car, accompanied by Junior's shrieks, careening the rest of the way to the basin floor. There was a solid crash as it hit bottom.

Up top, the crane pulled loose and Mark felt his cage drop with it.

In a tangle of cable and burning machinery, the entire platform rolled over the side.

Falling in stair-stepped increments, the crane unwound from its cables like a giant yo-yo, as it finally dropped all the way down onto the bottom.

Mark saw Rexy fall with it, even as his own cage dropped into free-fall.

He heard the impact rather than felt it when they all landed together.

Once the echo faded, there was a long silence in the basin.

Stretched beside the shallow river along the rocky bank, Rexy lay still.

A dozen feet away was the wreckage of the crane and Mark's cage.

Mark had no idea how long he lay there – minutes or seconds – he wasn't even sure if he had gone completely unconscious.

The wind had been knocked out of him and he remembered gasping, waiting to see if he would get his breath back or just simply suffocate, in chain-stoking chokes of broken ribs and punctured lungs.

But after a minute, he could breathe again.

He started to move experimentally, looking for the broken bones that *must* be there.

Miraculously, he found none.

"I think I'm okay," he said aloud, as if to test it.

Which proved not to be entirely the case as he sat up.

Maybe there were no breaks, but every bone in his body felt bruised. He groaned aloud, a miserable canine sound, as he twisted in the ruptured metal scrap of his cage.

The wreckage around him burned. He had landed close to the river, so the fire wasn't creeping yet. But that didn't mean things were done blowing up.

His cage was still locked, but the bars were bent. With his battered body objecting strenuously, Mark squeezed himself through.

Then he heard a pained moan from behind him.

Mark turned to where Rexy lay.

The pile of wreckage shifted as the beast tried to move.

But not this time.

She was broken, her limbs shattered – armor-piercing bullets had already turned her hide into chopped-meat, but the munitions left her a bloody ruin. That second LAW missile blast had taken away part of her tail.

Mark could see her eyes blinking, trying to focus.

Turning and focusing on *him*.

She let out another moan, choking and full of blood.

Mark turned back to the fallen chopper, stepping around pools of burning fuel. He approached cautiously, lest all that loose ammo start spontaneously firing.

He rummaged quickly through the cabin, averting his eyes from the crushed remains of the soldier manning the guns. In the cockpit, the pilot was burned unrecognizable.

Mark strapped the dead soldier's sidearm to his hip.

Then he slung an M-16 over his shoulder and approached Rexy for the last time.

He brought the barrel up to the suffering beast's head.

Rexy blinked back. One final groan escaped her – frustration? Even now?

"For what it's worth," Mark said, "I'm sorry."

He pulled the trigger. The blast actually threatened to knock him backwards. The burst of fire hit Rexy between both eyes, shattering the brain.

The big rex kicked once and was still.

In the moment of silence that followed, Mark actually mourned.

Then, behind him, there was an outraged squeal.

In the wreckage of the elevator, Junior stamped his one good leg, thrashing his tail, showing his teeth.

The little rex shrieked, its eyes meeting Mark's in that utterly unabashed way that wild things have.

It had just watched Mark shoot its mother.

Mark frowned, walking over to where the hatchling struggled, still trapped inside the elevator car, hopping on its cast.

Junior blinked back at him balefully.

Mark pulled the pistol from his hip, and aimed it at the little rex.

The blood of the little beast's mother still dotted his arms.

After a moment, he lowered the pistol, and pulled the door open.

Junior blinked, disbelieving. Then the little rex hopped up and out of the cage, struggling on its weak leg.

Mark held the gun ready, should the little beast attack – those teeth were nasty at five-pounds or five-tons.

But Junior just stared back. Then he turned and skittered off to the forest's edge.

The little creature paused, looking back, offering one last squeal, likely a curse. Then the little rex vanished into the brush.

Mark wondered if the hobbled leg would heal properly. Would the little beast survive?

And would it remember him?

He turned to the fallen carcass of the little rex' mother. He could smell where the fire had reached her and her flesh begun to burn.

For a full minute, Mark stood there silent, head down.

Then, from above, there was more gunfire and he heard voices.

Mark faded back, looking up. He could see spotlights shining down.

Rhodes was taking over. It was time to leave.

The spotlights focused on the wreckage, not the perimeter, probably attracted by the sound of Mark's own gunfire when he put Rexy down. But the spontaneous ammo fire that had already gone off provided a nice cover. They were clearly not looking for survivors – or escapees.

But as Mark skirted the edge of the forest, he had no idea that, once again, he had indeed been seen.

It was the woman in red. Standing at the precipice of the dam, she had seen him as he'd crawled from his cage.

She watched him put the big rex down. She saw him spare the hatchling.

More than anything in the world, she wanted to call his name.

But that was when the soldiers surrounded her with guns and blinding flashlights.

She felt hands upon her.

Sally shut her eyes as Mark disappeared into the forest and out of her life.

Again.

# CHAPTER 21

Mark knew someone was following him – at this point, his sixth-sense was like a combat-veteran's. But for now, he just wanted to run. He could not think of a single person or creature on Earth who he might be happy to see.

Most possible options were more like 'kill or be killed'.

Right at the moment, Mark wasn't sure he had another killing in him.

But as he heard the crack of brush behind him, someone giving chase, with no concern for stealth, Mark knew it wasn't going to be as simple as just being left alone.

Ironically, it was Rexy who finally allowed him to get angry.

As far as that big mama *T. rex* went, you could make a case he had it coming.

But, *that* debt was settled. Rexy's vendetta was done.

For whatever he might have owed that animal, he didn't owe anyone else a damn thing.

Mark pulled the pistol from his hip.

Maybe he had one more killin' in him today.

He stepped back deftly into the brush, something else that was becoming second nature – Rexy had left him a veritable ninja. He settled between the leaves, aiming his pistol back down the path he'd come.

After a moment, his pursuer came into view.

Mark cursed silently.

He stepped into the path as the running figure passed, body-checking her, and physically throwing her to the ground.

Lily rolled painfully in the dirt, her breath briefly knocked away. Then she looked up, her eyes wide, as Mark stood over her, with his gun drawn.

She made movements as if to skitter away, but Mark pulled back the hammer, and Lily grew still.

Mark took a deliberate breath.

"How the hell did you get down here?"

Lily swallowed.

"I… know lots of paths."

"Why are you following me, Lily?"

"I… wanted to say… I was sorry."

Mark choked out a bark of involuntary laughter.

"You're *sorry*?"

Mark honestly had nowhere to go with that – he *wanted* to say more, but could only just let the absurdity of it hang in the air.

Lily's eyes swelled with tears.

"I did what I had to… what I was *supposed* to…"

She looked up at him pleadingly.

"Oh, I get all that," Mark said, nodding. "Believe me, there's nothing here that I don't understand."

Lily blinked, letting the tears fall, and bringing her hand over her heart.

"But you *touched* me," she said helplessly.

Despite himself, Mark was still entranced by the sheer beauty of her dark eyes.

Experience was a wonderful thing – it allowed you to recognize the same mistakes every single damned time you made them.

Not this time.

“You touched me too,” Mark said.

He wiped his brow, still splattered with blood – he had no idea how much was his own.

“You left scars,” he said.

Lily’s eyes cast down.

“I didn’t want to,” she said.

“You still did it, though.”

She stared up at him, her eyes tearing pools.

Helpless as a hatchling *T. rex*.

But what might happen after she grows?

The thought of all of them on his tail, that whole crazy tribe – *Coven* – replacing a dragon with witches. And did he doubt they might be even as stubborn as Rexy herself?

They were, after all, *bad* witches.

Of course, that was assuming their tribe as a whole wasn’t acquired as 'assets' by Rhodes.

Either way, the only person who could tell anyone that *he* was still alive lay on the ground before him.

He wondered what another man would have done – what Rhodes would have – what Michelle, or Ginger, or even Lily herself would do.

But in the end, the only thing that really mattered was what *he* would do.

Mark thought of Sally.

He looked down at Lily, and brought the barrel of the pistol down to her head. She shrank back, cowering.

"I don't trust you," he said. "I would be an idiot to let you go."

Then he pulled the gun back, with a deep, resigned sigh.

Lily blinked up at him, her tears running freely.

For a bizarre moment, Mark actually felt the threat of tears himself.

Then, from above came the sound of choppers, still off in the distance.

Reinforcements. There were probably already troops on the ground, maybe even the basin floor.

He regarded Lily one last time.

"Goodbye, Lily," he said.

Mark turned, stepping into the trees, moving off the path, and began making his way down the slope.

Lily climbed to her feet, looking after him, but this time she didn't follow.

She was still standing there, when a spotlight from above found her and, in moments, she was surrounded by troops.

Lily didn't resist.

She did begin to cry.

And Mark, still less than two-hundred-meters down the slope, hidden invisibly among the trees, saw her taken.

Just like he had before, he stayed low as the spotlights searched past his cover among the trees.

But this time, when they had gone, he turned and went on his way.

He didn't look back.

# CHAPTER 22

Sally sat compliantly as the rest of the Coven was taken down around her. It was mostly over by the time the search crew brought in Lily.

As they led her past, Lily hung on Sally's eye, like a young girl with a shameful secret.

Sally let it pass – even after the end of the world, there were still a lot of those floating about.

But the train of thought faded quickly. She was still floating on full-dose narcotics. Only now, the spacey detachment seemed to help, as she took it all in stride, sitting calmly, hands cuffed, while the rest of the sisters were all rounded-up.

General Rhodes himself had landed with the reinforcements. He caught Sally's eye as he stepped out of the chopper.

She knew Rhodes' temper, and felt a touch of fear. But as he knelt beside her, his eyes were not angry. He ordered her cuffs removed.

"I'm glad to see you're alright, Miss Crawford," he said, in his old-school gentleman's manner. "I was worried about you."

Rhodes noted her dilated pupils, shaking his head disapprovingly, but he nodded reassuringly.

"It's alright. We'll talk later."

Some of the others gave them more trouble.

Christine emptied her pistol before being taken down, although she only actually killed two, including the LAW's gunner, and if you didn't count the chopper Rexy had brought down while the pilot was dodging her gunfire.

Michelle also gave them quite a fight. It was a lot like tackling a wildcat – she lashed out with teeth, claws, knees, elbows, sticks and rocks.

Finally, one of the soldiers, Lieutenant Hicks by his badge, with his eyes scratched and watering, his nose bloody, simply stepped forward and slugged her straight across her jaw with his full weight.

Michelle dropped bonelessly at his feet.

Luna, who had submitted to capture quietly up to this point, suddenly hissed, the scar on her cheek standing out starkly.

"*Bastard,*" she said, venomously, lashing out.

Hicks looked at his troop of four, tasked with taking down Michelle, all still writhing on the ground. Then he turned and slugged Luna too, dropping her beside Michelle, the scar on her face running with fresh blood.

Hicks' eyes turned to Ginger, sitting on her knees, next to her.

Ginger smiled disarmingly.

Hicks' eyes narrowed, but he said nothing as he wiped the blood from his face and escorted her aboard the chopper, laying her two unconscious companions on the seat beside her.

There were a couple of other skirmishes.

Serena took a stab at one of them with a knife secreted in her robe – a bit of a girlish attempt, and the soldier easily twisted the knife from her hand. Serena now sat in meek compliance, with most of the rest of the pledges, in their white robes.

They all kneeled before – kneeling now was an easy transition.

Rhodes surveyed the site, the available facilities, the damage to it – and of course, the new troop of *'refugees'* – perfect for the Arc-Project.

"Get them back to the Mount," Rhodes instructed Hicks.

Rhodes' eye turned towards a last lone figure, still cloaked in red, sitting separate from the others.

"You need to come with us too, Miss Crawford," the General said. "We've got to get you someplace safe."

He touched a hand on her shoulder.

"After all, you are our most valuable resource."

Sally said nothing but the bitter sting of tears touched her eye.

She looked down at the forest where she had watched Mark disappear for the second time.

And for the second time, there was something she wished she could have told him.

Back on the base that day, the medics had figured out why she'd been getting sick recently. It was actually kind of a no-brainer, she thought, with just a touch of chagrin.

And after the first couple months, she was only just now beginning to show.

Sally ran her hand under her robe, over the barely perceptible bulge in her stomach.

General Rhodes came to see her the day after the medics reported the news. He told her then the same thing he told her now – she had just become the 'most valuable asset to the human race'.

“You're going to give us the next generation,” he said.

Rhodes had smiled.

In a way, that smile had been what caused her to run. Perhaps now, it was the reason she stayed.

Maybe she could escape again, track down Mark in the prehistoric wilderness.

But most likely, she couldn’t. Not on her own.

And a post-apocalyptic waste was no place to raise a child. In that light, perhaps the offer of survival and security was worth her freedom.

Sally held her hand over her stomach.

She hoped so.

Hands touched her shoulders.

“Come along, ma’am,” Lieutenant Hicks said, turning her towards the chopper.

Sally turned to follow, allowing herself to be herded with the rest.

# CHAPTER 23

The fire in the basin eventually burned itself out.

In the bushes along the river, a little *T. rex* watched as a bunch of walking apes dissected his mother.

Junior had hidden in the area most of the day, unwilling to leave her body behind.

But now, as the hairless apes brought out their knives and chainsaws, he faded back into the brush.

He had gnawed away his cast and now he stood, wobbling slightly on his hobbled leg. As he walked, he demonstrated a pronounced limp.

But *T. rex* was a hardy beast, and the leg had been well-set. Given time, he would heal. Settling into an awkward lope, Junior left the basin behind.

And while one could debate the intellect of this little creature, it would not be unreasonable to suspect that he carried the image of his dead mother with him.

Certainly, he remembered the scents that were left behind. And like his mother, he responded to them instinctively. That was what passed for thought.

And just like his mother, Junior separated Mark from all the rest.

It was an olfactory memory that would stay with him forever.

And as he caught the scent, instinct dictated his response.

The trail lay ahead.

Nose to the ground like a bloodhound, the little rex began to follow.

**END of BOOK TWO**

Check out other great

# Dinosaur Thrillers!

Julian Michael Carver

## TRIASSIC

After spending many years in artificial hypersleep, a handful of survivors of the exploration vessel Supernova awaken to find their ship torn to shreds. They are unsure of what happened in space or how they crashed into an uncharted planet. Upon exploration of the new world, they soon realize their destination: The Triassic, the first chapter of the Mesozoic Era. A plan is formulated to escape this terrifying landscape plagued with dinosaurs and prehistoric beasts. The survivors soon discover that there may be an even larger threat looming under the trees than just the dinosaurs, threatening to cut their mission short and trap them all forever in the primitive depths of the Triassic.

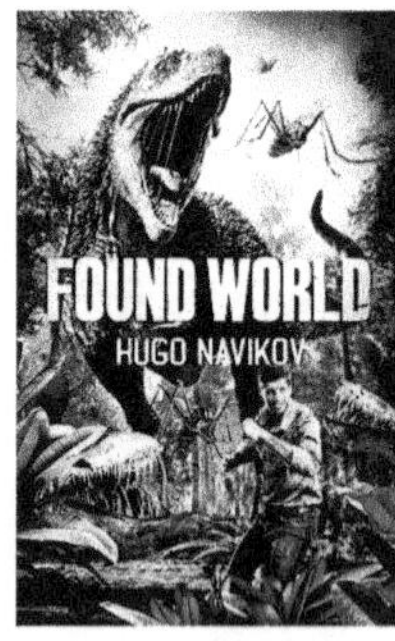


Hugo Navikov

## THE FOUND WORLD

A powerful global cabal wants adventurer Brett Russell to retrieve a superweapon stolen by the scientist who built it. To entice him to travel underneath one of the most dangerous volcanoes on Earth to find the scientist, this shadowy organization will pay him the only thing he cares about: information that will allow him to avenge his family's murder. But before he can get paid, he and his team must enter an underground hellscape of killer plants, giant insects, terrifying dinosaurs, and an army of other predators never previously seen by man. At the end of this journey awaits a revelation that could alter the fate of mankind ... if they can make it back from this horrifying found world.

Check out other great

# Dinosaur Thrillers!

Gustavo Bondoni

## TEST SITE HORROR

Lieutenant Max Alexeyev is a Russian Special Forces soldier. His job is to protect his country's interests at home and abroad, not to rescue overly ambitious reporters who have bitten off stories too big to chew. But when his unit gets called to a press event at a laboratory that has been invaded by dinosaurs, that's exactly what he finds himself doing. Fighting both prehistoric nightmares and the products of modern genetic experiments in the forests of the Ural Mountains, he battles for his own survival as well as that of alluring journalist Marianne Caruso and her peers.Unbeknownst to him, however, shadowy human forces are at work to ensure that no one spills the secrets of the research being done in the area.Will they live to tell the story of the Test Site Horror?

John Lee Schneider

## AGE OF MONSTERS

Once upon a time, Dinosaurs ruled the Earth.But the Mesozoic era – the Age of Reptiles – came to its cataclysmic end sixty-five million years ago.The Age of Monsters begins tonight.And the world of humankind will crumble. Some will call it Judgment. Some will attempt to fight. Others will simply run. Most will just try and survive. But no one will escape.In the mountains. In the oceans. In the cities and towns. Even up in space.Where were YOU when the world ended?

Check out other great

# Dinosaur Thrillers!

Steve Metcalf

## OBJEKT 221

Ruthless multi-national conglomerate Allied Genetics is under siege from a paramilitary force for hire. Allied calls in reinforcements and fortifies their crown-jewel property – an abandoned Soviet military facility in Crimea known during the Cold War as Objekt 221. Fortunately for the future of their research, O221 straddles a stretch of rocky landscape that hides a rift – a portal through time and space. Through this rift, Allied Genetics can travel, at will, to the Cretaceous – 100 million years into Earth's past – and bolster their genetic experiments with dinosaur DNA ... something their competitors want to stop at all costs."Objekt 221" is a story blending numerous science fiction elements such as repurposed military facilities, time travel, rogue corporate armies, dinosaurs and the hint of a super-ancient civilization.

Bestselling collection

## PREHISTORIC: A DINOSAUR ANTHOLOGY

PREHISTORIC is an action packed collection of stories featuring terrifying creatures that once ruled the Earth. Lost worlds where T-Rex and Velociraptors still roam and man is now on the menu. Laboratories at the forefront of cloning technology experiment with dinosaurs they do not understand or are able to contain. The deepest parts of the ocean where Megalodon, the largest and most ferocious predator to have ever existed is stalking new prey. Plus many more thrillers filled with extinct prehistoric monsters written by some of the best creature feature authors this side of the Jurassic period.

www.ingramcontent.com/pod-product-compliance
Lightning Source LLC
Chambersburg PA
CBHW072239190626
46809CB00018B/2852

* 9 7 8 1 9 2 2 8 6 1 8 8 7 *